LOTTERY OF SECRETS
A PSYCHOLOGICAL THRILLER WITH A SHOCKING TWIST

NADIJA MUJAGIC

Copyright © 2023 by Nadija Mujagic

All rights reserved.

No part of this book may be reproduced in any form or by any electronic or mechanical means, including information storage and retrieval systems, without written permission from the author, except for the use of brief quotations in a book review.

This is a work of fiction. Names, characters, places, and incidents either are the product of the author's imagination or are used fictitiously, and any resemblance of actual persons, living or dead, businesses, companies, events, or locales is entirely coincidental.

A Thriller

LOTTERY
OF
SECRETS

*A jackpot won
A nightmare begun*

NADIJA
MUJAGIC

CHAPTER 1

I'D RATHER DIE than let Jimmy discover my lottery win. I wouldn't be able to get the words out to tell anyone about it anyway, because this can't be happening. I must be having an incredible dream, one I never want to wake up from.

But it's all too real.

"Holy crap," I whisper to myself.

The scratch ticket feels smooth in my hand, and I just keep turning it over and over; reading it, caressing it.

Five million dollars.

How do I even begin to grapple with that? It's been a while since I won anything. All my recent winnings have been miniscule—ten dollars here and there, just enough to pay for the ticket, and a little extra for a cup of coffee.

But this? This is just crazy. I'd never in a million years believe that I, Lynn Miller, could win this amount of money, just with a simple scratch ticket. My lucky stars have finally shone upon me.

After the disheartening news I received the other day, I

thought to myself: "Why not indulge in a bit of enjoyment and try my luck with a few scratch tickets?"

I fidget in the front seat of my car and hold the ticket up in the air in front of me, shaking it. I sniff it and bring it closer to my eyes to check the three matching amounts again. It's not a dream; it's most definitely real. Even so, I count all the zeroes, one-two-three-four-five-six, that precede a five, and I force myself to catch a breath and hold it to stop myself from hyperventilating.

Five million dollars in three slots. I count the zeroes yet again, my hands shaking as I cross my fingers over the ticket. My belly hasn't stirred with this much excitement in a long time, if ever.

But I put a lid on the euphoria and stifle it because it won't last. It just can't.

I start to turn on the engine, and a sudden surge of coughing catches me by surprise, overwhelming me. I get out of my car, walk to the passenger side, and bend down near a bush. Clots of blood spew out of my mouth and settle on the grass beside the bush. My knees buckle under the strain of my weak body, so I kneel on the ground and take time to slow my breathing and compose myself. These little attacks I've been having as of late are becoming more violent and frequent, and there's not a lot I can do to tame them. I wipe my mouth and head back to the car.

It's an old Honda Acord I've kept alive, thanks to Jimmy, who's an experienced car mechanic. But now I can afford to buy a new one and not worry about whether it will get me into an accident like the one I had a few years ago. I'm still shaken from that experience, and I always drive extra carefully to avoid a mishap. The driver's door is still jangly, but I've learned to yank it hard every time I open and close it.

When I sit down, I realize I'd left the ticket on the passenger's seat while I was busy coughing up my insides, and I cuss at myself for being stupid and careless. Who leaves five million dollars lying around? Me, apparently. I'm being paranoid, though. No one could have stolen it. After all, I'm sitting in a deserted restaurant parking lot when it's too late for lunch and too early for dinner.

I slam the door shut and do a frantic search in my mind for places to run away to. Jimmy has a tight leash on me, but maybe—just maybe—this is my ticket to freedom.

As I drive to the house, I daydream about what I can do with the five million dollars in my hands. A new, big house with a swimming pool, a luxurious car, and a fancy vacation. I have never left New England, and I'd love to see places like Atlantic City or Las Vegas. Do a little gambling, have some fun. Or maybe go to Bahamas or Bermuda. Frankly, I don't know the difference between these two, but I've heard they're both exotic. Who cares about the difference? It's a place to get a suntan and savor new kinds of food.

But who am I kidding? I'm not going anywhere. I won't be spending this money on a new lavish lifestyle or any brand-new persona this money can buy. None of these options are ultimately viable. I know exactly what this money can do for me. It won't be any fancy houses, cars, vacations: none of that.

It will have to be spent on a good cause. Something worthy enough to bring me redemption, erase the guilt I've carried all these years.

Only then I can die in peace.

CHAPTER 2

WHEN I GET HOME, I sigh with relief that Jimmy's car is missing from our driveway. He must still be at work. It will buy me enough time to hide the ticket and come up with a plan.

I park in front of our house, noticing more than ever that it looks like a shithole. The conditions are more noticeable now I could have a better option. Now that I'm picturing that big house with a swimming pool.

We rented it so long ago that the landlord no longer minds if we can't pay the rent on time. Jimmy brings this up whenever he doesn't want to pay his half of the rent because he's in a bad mood about his life. I take a couple of extra shifts at the restaurant to make enough to cover for his half. I'm surprised the landlord hasn't kicked us out yet, but I'm sure he appreciates our predictability and the fact he doesn't have to do any major repairs, even though the house needs them.

It's in a row of other similarly looking homes, all one

story high and piled in close together. Rose, our nosy older neighbor, is on one side, and a young couple we rarely see on the other. The house's location is prime, just a few blocks from the beach. But it's small, the size of a shoe box. Jimmy and I spend most of our time apart when we're in the house—me in the bedroom, and he on the couch in the living room.

We've slept separately for decades. It's one of those things you don't think about twice. You just do it, because it's become second nature and if it suddenly reversed, it would just be too weird. Unnatural.

When I enter the house, it's quiet except for the fridge humming in the kitchen's corner. It's an old GL fridge, often leaking from underneath and stuffed with beer and vodka, Jimmy's favorite. A musty smell has lingered inside the house. We ever barely open the windows to air out the space. The walls are crumbling, and the paint has chipped, hanging from the ceiling, but we've had no means to fix any of it.

We don't call the landlord to complain or request repairs, for the fear he will kick us out. Because if he did, I don't think we could find a better place for the same price. Our credit scores or references are not exactly what you'd consider favorable. That's why, when the roof leaked recently, Jimmy fixed it himself, with large sheets of nylon bags secured with bricks. The leaks have dwindled, but they're still there. At least the roof hasn't collapsed on us yet.

It's our home, but it doesn't always feel welcoming or

warm. Inside, there isn't one photograph of Jimmy and me together hanging on the wall or sitting on top of the dressers or side tables. No memorabilia or trinkets that tie us to our past. You'd think there would be at least a damn fridge magnet from a place we'd visited together, but not even that. The house is plain, boring, and tired-looking, reminding me of all the things that got us where we are now.

We have let the house go, just like we've let go of our marriage and ourselves.

Now that I've won a lot of money, we could get out of this situation and find a better home, one more suitable for our tastes. All these years, Jimmy has dreamt of having a large yard overlooking the ocean, where we can spread out and have BBQs on a whim. Invite people to ooohh and aaahh at our beautiful life. This house is not conducive to happy living.

I wish I could be excited to share the news with Jimmy about the win. I wish I could get caught up in the joy of the dream alongside him, as we planned for our new home. But I've made myself a promise, and I don't want to get his hopes up just to dash them.

The first thing I do when I come inside is take the winning ticket out of my bra and put it under the mattress of my bed. I am pretty certain Jimmy won't go into my room, much less snoop around. There's no way he'd suspect I'd just won the lottery.

I wrack my brain and try to plan my next steps. I pace the living room, my mind racing. What have I seen winners do in the past when they're on the news? Nothing comes to mind. I guess I should keep my mouth shut for now and maybe find a lawyer. But I don't know any. I've only heard of some guy Jimmy threatened me with as a divorce lawyer years ago, when, in reality, he was just a clerk in the town court. Those threats came and went, over and over, and I'm just numb to them now.

There's no doubt I could find a lawyer on the internet. Under normal circumstances, I'd also need an accountant to help me manage the incoming wealth. But my circumstances are anything but normal.

All my life, I've dealt mainly with cash. The tips I've earned from waitressing and some gambling at the main casino in Hampton, a hole in the wall I used to call my second home. Jimmy forbade me from going there ages ago. He said vices like gambling are not for poor people like us. When I mentioned his heavy drinking, he explained that it was just a welcome reprieve from his busy day from work, and not a vice.

I lie down on the couch, albeit restlessly, and place my head on the headboard, a position that helps me manage my breathing. To reduce the anxiety caused by today's news, I take a few deep breaths and close my eyes.

My job comes to mind. I've worked at the same restaurant, Red Urchin, for many years and I can't help but consider what it would be like just to quit. Barbara may need me, since the tourist season is about to bloom, and it's been difficult finding staff that won't quit on a whim. I don't want to let Barbara down, but leaving could be the best option, especially as I have little time left. The heaviness of all the thinking lulls me to sleep.

The slamming of the front door pulls me from my slumber. I look up at the clock on the wall and see it's past seven. Jimmy stumbles into the room, swaying from side to side like a tree, and doing his best not to fall. The heavy smell of alcohol fills the room.

I stand up and sit straight on the couch, feeling woozy from the sleep.

Jimmy stops in the middle of the room and stares at me. "What the hell have you been doing all afternoon?"

For some reason, he doesn't believe taking naps during the day is an acceptable activity. His voice sounds harsh and intimidating. I've heard it many times, and I know what comes next. More intimidation and interrogation.

"I fell asleep." I shrug. "I didn't mean to."

He rests his eyes on the kitchen, a few feet away from where he's standing. "Anything to eat?"

"I don't know," I say. "Look in the cabinet."

Most days, Barbara kindly allows me to take a plate or two of food from the restaurant, but today I was too distracted and forgot to bring some home. I haven't cooked in a while. Jimmy has never been impressed with my culinary skills, which I can't blame him for to be honest. They're nearly nonexistent. Sometimes I wonder if that's one reason I've kept the waitressing job as long as I have. Getting free meals on a regular is a good benefit.

Jimmy stands in the middle of the room, his menacing

eyes looking at me. His fists clench and unclench by his sides and his jaw tightens. "What did you say?"

He hates being told to do something, even when it's only for his benefit.

"I said, look in the cabinet. There's some noodle soup you can put in the microwave. Sorry, I forgot to get some food at Urchin."

As always, I don't mean to enrage Jimmy, but I fully expect what comes next. It happens pretty much every single time he drinks. He stomps in my direction, then his feet land in front of me. He raises his right arm and swings it above me, and the next thing I know his hand is slapping my face hard, sending vibrations through my head.

I don't flinch. I've felt worse.

He stares down at me and waits for my reaction. I do and say nothing. I put my head down to compose my thoughts, then bring it back up to gaze at Jimmy's tired eyes.

"I won the lottery." As soon as I blurt it out, I bite down on my lip and clench my fists. My eyes roll in my sockets, regretting it the second the words come out of my mouth. The cat is out of the bag, and there's no way to beckon it back. I didn't tell Jimmy to make him happy, I was just hoping it would distract him, and then maybe he'll skip the beating tonight. There's more of it to come. A single slap is always just a prelude.

His head cocks to the side, and he narrows his eyes at me. "Huh?"

"I won the lottery today. Five million dollars."

"Are you fucking with me?" He stares down at me with disgust on his face.

I jump up from the couch and run to the bedroom. Under the mattress, I feel for the ticket and pull it out, gripping it as if my life depends on it. And maybe it does. I walk back to the living room, where Jimmy's still standing in the same spot. His mouth is hanging open, and he looks agitated, unsure of what he'd just heard.

I hand him the ticket. "Here."

He looks at me with distrust on his face and yanks the ticket out of my hand. He brings it closer to his eyes, as if waiting for the image to travel to his brain so he can fully register the news.

"Holy shit. Five mill!" Jimmy looks at me and lets an uproarious laugh. "We're rich. We're damn filthy rich."

I imagine a thousand new possibilities flash in front of his eyes. The news sobers him up, and joy covers his face. He approaches me and picks me up with ease—a mere hundred and twenty pounds is nothing for Jimmy. He swings me around a few times, then drops me on the floor and pushes me away. His gaze is fixed on the ticket as he grins.

I sigh in relief. I wasn't meaning to make Jimmy happy, but I've avoided the beating, although I know I deserve it. Tonight, I'm just too weak to take it. Tonight, I need a break.

CHAPTER 3

AS I HOPED, Jimmy's mood shifts like the seasons and he leaves me alone tonight. His violent stupor doesn't happen too often; only when he has a stressful day and too much to drink. All these years, I've availed myself to him like a rag doll he uses as a punching target. It really isn't so bad. I can usually live with it, but tonight is an exception. I'm not feeling well, and I'm overwhelmed by all the things I need to get done.

Jimmy, ever since he'd learned about the winning, hasn't shut up about it. All night, he's been yapping about his plans to quit his job soon. His words make me shudder. If Jimmy wasn't working, he'd dick around, doing nothing around the house and drinking even more.

And there's another reason of course: Jimmy won't see a penny.

"I don't need to be a grease monkey anymore, Lynn. No more dealing with shitty people and telling them to take care of their car. I mean, that's good for the business, but how these assholes don't care to change oil every five thousand miles is beyond me."

He takes a sip of his beer and frowns. He gazes over at me, as if expecting me to say something, but I keep silent. I've got too much on my mind.

I turn the TV on and settle in the recliner in front of the set. I flip through the channels, and usually, Jimmy directs me to slow down or to stop on a channel, but this time he doesn't. He looks to be on cloud nine, deep in delirious thought, and I can tell he is thinking of all the possibilities of a better life.

Now, he's bound to have moved on to daydream about living in a mansion, overlooking an enormous green lawn, decorated with hedges and flowers, and the ocean just beyond that. Houses like that sit on the other side of the hill just a few short blocks away from us. It's a startlingly different world. We live in proximity to one of the most excellent beaches in the United States, bringing thousands of people around every year, and the real estate properties that overlook the stunning sandy beaches and the ocean are priced in millions.

Owning one of those houses has only ever been a dream that could now easily become a reality. Whenever Jimmy spots one on the market, he cusses out the people who can afford to buy them.

But now he is one of those people, or so he thinks.

"I'm going to look for an agent to help us buy a new house."

I flinch at his announcement, every nerve in my body tensing.

"Isn't it too early?" I ask, injecting a casual tone into my words.

"Too early for what?"

"To call an agent. I need to sort out the ticket first and get the money. Plus, I don't know how long it's going to take."

He waves at me and shakes his head. "It's never too early to check out houses."

Predictably, Jimmy is all about what he can do with the money. My plans for it don't include him, but I need to keep him convinced that he'll benefit, and it's going to take every ounce of strength to keep the truth from him.

After the laundry list of what our life could become, anywhere from owning fancy cars to top-of-the-line clothes, to elaborate vacations, he turns to me and lifts a beer bottle in his right hand, pointing it at me. "And you ... you can finally fix those crooked teeth of yours." Jimmy laughs.

"What are you saying about my teeth?" His words sting, but to tell him that is pointless. I remember the days when he thought of me as the prettiest girl alive, but those days are long gone.

"Don't be mad, darling. I'm just helping you out."

The word "darling" makes me wince. I don't remember the last time Jimmy called me a pet name. Jimmy lifts the sleeve of his shirt and looks at his biceps. He is fit and all muscle. He is a man's man through and through, and he wants everyone to know it. "Maybe it's time to get a new tattoo," he says. "What do you think, Lynn? Right here, a big one across the whole fucking arm."

I briefly gaze at him and turn to the TV. I pretend to concentrate on watching *Family Feud*, but Jimmy doesn't shut up.

"Maybe I can get an angel holding a cigar, or maybe a truck and a Bentley side by side."

These are the dumbest ideas for tattoos, but I won't say anything. Jimmy would ignite like a fire and strike. I hold my gaze on the TV and ignore him.

"Hey. Are you listening?" His voice is loud and irritated.

"I'm trying to watch the TV. Can you be quiet already?"

He takes the remote from the coffee table in front of him and turns the volume up as loudly as it can go. "How about now? Is this good?" He is shouting to compete against the voices on TV.

It's difficult to reason with him on anything, including the TV volume, when he's drunk. I stand up from the recliner and rush to the bedroom. As soon as I enter, the TV volume is down again. I tap my back pocket and feel the lottery ticket. Tonight, I won't be hiding it under the mattress. I'll put it in a place no one can ever dream of finding. The last thing I want is for Jimmy to take it and claim it as his own.

There's a little slot in the wall, a crack of sorts, that Jimmy has never repaired. I've mentioned it to him several times, but he forgets about it. We had a family of mice enter the house a couple of years ago, and since then, I've been wary of any holes that can bring creatures from the outside. Fixing the hole is not Jimmy's priority. I notice it only because I know it's there; otherwise, it's well disguised.

I tuck the ticket inside the hole and place a sticky over it. Then I think better of it and remove the sticky, afraid it might draw attention. With nothing better to do, I drop into the bed and outline my next steps. Tomorrow morning, at the crack of dawn, I'm going to search for a lawyer.

CHAPTER 4

IN THE MORNING, I wake up to the ocean sounds and birds chirping outside. The turbulent waves in the distance is one thing I never tire of. It lulls me to a calm, but I can't stay in bed all day. I have important things to do. The ticket is still in the crack, just as I left it last night. I pull it out carefully and kiss it, like it's a life-saving token.

I peer into the living room, where I find Jimmy snoring on the couch. He's lying on his back, his mouth wide open, and his left arm resting on his forehead. I hope he'll stay in that position, sleeping for a while, as I don't want him to question my departure from the house. I tiptoe back to the bedroom to put on my denim shorts and a sweatshirt. The ticket goes into the inside pocket of my purse.

In the living room, Jimmy makes a slight commotion in his sleep, then turns around and continues to snore.

I sneak by him slowly for the exit.

The morning feels unusually cold, but it promises another sunny day. I head toward the beach and walk by the houses, none of which are showing any signs of life yet. The sun is inching up from the horizon, sprinkling its rays across the wavy ocean, a beautiful sight of life and energy. It's only six o'clock and Hampton Beach is ghostly. But in less than a couple of hours, it will hop with locals and tourists.

I sit on a bench, pull a pack of cigarettes out of my sweatshirt pocket and light one. It's been a while since I smoked. My emotions have taken me on a rollercoaster since the second I saw the numbers on that winning ticket yesterday. I'm still a bundle of nerves, numbness and, excitement. Cigarettes have always been my rescue in the past. But I highly doubt I will enjoy them like I used to back in the day. I deeply inhale, feel dizzy, and close my eyes. Seconds later, the cough catches me off guard, and my whole body convulses. I get up with difficulty and catch the railings separating the beach from the sidewalk. I bend over the railing and let the blood clots travel through my throat until they land on the sand. The process of coughing it all up exhausts me.

An older man walks by with a leashed dog and asks if I am okay while I'm bent over the railing. I tell him it's nothing. The dog sniffs me, then approaches the lit cigarette on the ground, and retrieves immediately. I apologize to the man and step on the cigarette with all my might.

I sit back down on the bench and watch the man walk away with his dog. From the back pocket of my shorts, I extract my phone. I've never been in a situation where I've needed to look for an attorney, so I do the only thing that occurs to me. I scroll to the Yelp app and start my search. I type in "lawyer for lottery" in the box on the top, and within seconds, hundreds of results come out. There are so many lawyers out there. I pick the very first one on the top of my search results. The attorney's office is rated at three stars overall, but it seems to be close by. I click on the phone number next to the name, expecting the voice mail to pick up. Instead, a woman's voice answers, "Hello?"

She sounds surprised that someone would call this early in the morning as I am that someone would pick up. But I've heard lawyers put in an insane number of hours a day, so maybe it's not that strange.

"I need a lawyer." I get straight to the point. My voice sounds urgent, but I think I'm just nervous.

"Okay. That's me." The voice on the other side sounds confident.

"Okay. Well, we need to meet as soon as possible."

"Can you tell me what this is in regard to?"

"Sure. Yesterday, I won five million with a scratch ticket," I say. "Now I need help to cash it out and plan the next steps."

"Firstly, congratulations," the woman says cheerfully. "I can definitely help you with this. How about we meet in my office today at noon?"

"Sure." I don't know if it's usually easy to find a lawyer this quickly, or whether my new wealth has something to do with it, but I'm relieved I've found someone to represent me. She tells me the exact location of her office, which I commit to my memory.

"And don't forget to bring the ticket," she says.
"I won't."

We hang up and I stand up immediately before walking over to the railing. I look beyond the ocean and I'm flooded with memories. The days I used to swim at five in the morning when no soul would dare show up, are now over for me. My strength left me long ago and I'm getting too frail for such activities. For the same reason, I can't wait to walk into the restaurant and tell Barbara I quit. But I will wait a day or two until I'm sure the money is in my pocket.

When I arrive home, Jimmy is still sleeping, his back turned to me. It looks like he hasn't moved at all, and I'm relieved. He's no longer snoring, but his breathing is heavy and skips beats. He should be waking up soon and going to work. I walk straight to the bedroom and open the small closet in the corner of my room. It's stuffed with clothes I rarely wear, and the floor has piles and piles of stuff I haven't touched in ages. Old duffel bags, tennis rackets, sweatshirts, T-shirts, a snorkeling gear.

The blue blanket I have kept for decades.

It's safely tucked in a plastic bag in the closet's corner. Sometimes I smell it and imagine what it would be like to have used it.

I snap out of my thoughts and force myself not to think about it. I shuffle through the clothes hanging on the rod and look for the best suit or dress to wear for the occasion today. Over the past year, I've lost significant weight—over fifty pounds—so it wouldn't surprise me if most of these clothes hang on me like old rags on a scarecrow.

The blue dress sitting between two shirts draws my eyes. I remember buying it many moons ago, when Greta was getting married. Greta was a close friend who stuck by me in high school. We were odd ducks against the other classmates, the two girls who couldn't care less about submitting their homework on time. Greta still did well, despite her lack of diligence at school. She got a bachelor's degree at a community college and dated a guy with a decent job who finally proposed and married her. Jimmy and I showed up at the wedding, a young married couple ourselves. Jimmy got so drunk that he started to scream and throw glasses against the floor.

It was the first time I saw Jimmy's propensity for violence. While it surprised me, I didn't think much of it at the time. Everybody gets a little feisty when under the influence.

Right?

We got kicked out of their wedding promptly. I was too embarrassed to face Greta again, not even to apologize. Maybe that's not a bad thing. It would have been hard to witness her happy marriage while mine was rotting and falling to pieces.

Maybe the blue dress isn't a good idea after all.

I run my hand through the clothes and find a yellow shirt that I've always loved, but had no opportunities to wear. I felt great about how I looked the last time I wore it.

I pick up a black pair of slacks and settle on this combination.

Before I can place it on the bed to let it sit and air out, Jimmy startles me by appearing at the door. His eyes are heavy and sleepy.

"Oh my God, you scared the shit out of me," I say.

"What are you doing?"

"Nothing."

"What do you mean 'nothing'? How could you be doing nothing when you're doing something?"

I'm quiet for a moment, staring at Jimmy, waiting for a full blow. He trots over to me and grabs my arms, staring back at me. A lump is slowly traveling down my throat and I'm shaking inside, but I try not to let Jimmy smell my fear.

"Come here, baby-face."

I flinch, as his wave of affection shocks me. He takes my hand and gently pulls me toward the bed. I'm leaning on the edge, and he pushes me hard, causing me to land awkwardly and hit my head hard against the headboard. Pain shoots through me, but I say nothing. It wouldn't make any difference.

"You're so sexy when you're rich. You know that?" He's talking through clenched teeth, and I can feel his spittle land on my face. His breathing is manic, and his hands are all over me, attempting to rid me of my clothes.

I'd hate for Jimmy to think that having sex will make a difference in our marriage. He takes my clothes off and gently kisses my abs. His touch feels unnatural. It's been a while since we were intimate or touched each other with the intention of having sex, and it doesn't feel good at all. In fact, I hate it.

I spread my legs and arms on the bed, close my eyes and clench my teeth. I do nothing else, just wait for this terrible mistake to pass.

CHAPTER 5

WHEN JIMMY IS DONE, he gets up and goes to the bathroom. Shamefully, I turn to my side and bring my legs up to my chin. I feel empty and cheap, and resentful at Jimmy for initiating sex after so many months, years. I'd forgotten how it feels, and now I wish I hadn't been reminded.

Jimmy is talking to himself in the bathroom. I wonder how he feels about us having sex after all this time. If he expects me to oblige from now on, he's mistaken. I'd craved Jimmy's physical touch for so long, but now that touch repulses me. I have no desire to connect with him on a physical level. On *any* level.

Like my mind, the bed is in disarray. My yellow shirt is on the floor, crumbled into a ball. I squint my eyes hard and picture punching Jimmy's face. That's the one thing I've dreamt of doing on a daily basis, but the price to pay would be too high. He comes out of the bathroom and goes to the kitchen to make coffee. He's whistling, which means he is happy and satisfied.

"Lynn!" he yells out of the kitchen, but I could hear him just as well if he spoke at a normal level. The space is compact, and the sounds travel easily. "Do we have any Half & Half?"

"I don't know. Look in the fridge."

The fridge door screeches open, and he yells out, "I don't see any. Fuck! Didn't I tell you to get it yesterday?"

I remember nothing about yesterday. The sight of those winning number combinations has overshadowed all the other events of the day. I remain quiet because I don't want to provoke any more rage.

"Damn it, Lynn, you're useless!" He slams the fridge door, then walks into the living room. It's amazing how fleeting and short-lasting his happiness is. His belt jangles as he puts his pants on. He mutters under his breath, then leaves the house, slamming the door behind him.

That we just had sex means nothing to him. It just takes one thing he disapproves of, and he's back to his normal self, belligerent and self-entitled.

I'm surprised he hasn't asked me about how I'm going to cash the ticket or when. For that, I am grateful. Come to think of it, Jimmy has always been about his immediate needs, his tunnel vision always winning out.

This is the reason I've stopped telling him all the important things in my life. Like my declining health.

Yet, Jimmy must have surely observed the marked decline

in my appearance, the rapid weight loss that has gripped me in such a brief span. If he did, though, he chose not to broach the subject, opting not to voice his apprehension for the woman he's shared three decades of his life with, a woman who he could potentially lose. However, I don't hold him accountable, as in truth, hardly anyone else has come forward to acknowledge the profound change in my well-being and express their genuine concern for my distressing condition.

Merely a week ago, my doctor delivered the devastating diagnosis of lung cancer. While she refrained from divulging a prognosis regarding my remaining time, I can't help but mentally allocate myself a mere two fleeting months, if fate should prove merciful. Perhaps it's an exaggeration, but that's the weight of it, the inexorable sensation that now envelops me.

Even if there exists a silent suspicion that my health teeters on the precipice of peril, no one ever dares to utter or inquire about that dreaded word – "cancer."

About six months ago, I'd coughed up some nasty bloody stuff, and the naïve me thought it was from the long-lasting effect of chain-smoking when I was younger. I'd quit smoking many years ago, but the cancer snuck up on me unexpectedly. If I'd had a better health insurance, I would have gone to see my doctor a lot sooner. But I don't have any. Neither does Jimmy. Private health insurance is still optional, and we can't afford it.

Now I'm about to have millions of dollars, it's too late to seek treatment that I can afford. The cancer has metastasized and spread into my bones. Surprisingly, I feel I've had enough time to fully embrace my mortality. Facing my death is difficult, but I feel privileged to have been selected to exist in this world and the cosmos. Life: I can't think of a better gift in the world.

Ultimately, I don't mind dying soon. But the cancer complicates things with the lottery even more. Jimmy can't find out about my impending demise.

He hasn't returned home by the time I leave the house, which suits me well. He's probably at work and should be back between six and eight tonight, depending on whether he chooses to go drinking after work. I don't feel like explaining to him why I'm dressed differently today, or who I'm meeting. I leave my car in our driveway and walk to the lawyer's office. All these years, I've never expected to be visiting an attorney's office, and it's just a short walk from our home.

Sometimes I think about what else could hide in this small town.

When I arrive, my heart rate picks up. I grasp my purse closer to my body, remembering that I've safely stuffed my ticket in there. The sign across the front door is impossible to miss. LIBBY AND LIBBY, ESQ.

I take some hesitant steps forward and knock on the glass door. After feeling silly for knocking, I open up the door and enter the elegant office space, taking in the soft music in the background and the artwork featuring the ocean a million different ways hung on the walls. A young woman behind the front desk is talking on the phone and diverts her eyes from me as soon as our gazes meet. I'm standing in the middle of the floor awkwardly when the office door opens up and a young woman peeks through the gap.

"You must be the lottery winner." She's wearing a suit and sporting a bobcat haircut, which doesn't look great on her long face. Yet, her features are soft and friendly, and they put me at ease. "Come in."

I follow her and enter her enormous office overlooking the beach. "Wow, that's quite the view," I say.

She smiles. "Right? I've worked so hard for this, and it better be worth it."

I've worked hard all my life, and what do I have? A shoe box and a shitty husband making my life miserable. But that's all about to change, I suppose.

"Have a seat." She extends her arm to the oval table in the corner of her office. "Would you like something to drink? Coffee? Tea? Water?"

"No, thanks. Actually... can I have coffee, please?"

"Absolutely." She approaches the interphone on her desk, pushes the button and says, "Emily, can you bring my client a cup of coffee?" She turns back to me. "Anything with it?"

"No. Black please."

"Black." She releases the button and walks up to the table. "So, congratulations again. You must be very excited, Mrs...." She pauses and raises eyebrows. I realize we haven't made formal introductions yet. She doesn't know my name, nor do I know hers. Money is our connection, and it's strong enough to ignore all else.

"Mrs. Miller. Lynn Miller. You can call me Lynn."

"Nice to meet you, Lynn. You can call me Sam, short for Samantha."

I nod. She doesn't strike me as a Samantha, but I digress.

"Nice to meet you."

"So, tell me. Where did you buy the scratch ticket?" She widens her eyes, and they look giant against her small and pointy head.

"At the convenience store down the street."

"Isn't that in-cre-di-ble."

"Yes. Yes, quite incredible," I say.

"I'm happy to help you navigate claiming the ticket and setting up the next steps. I'm assuming you have the ticket with you?"

"Yes, I have it on me." I open up my purse and pull it out from the safety of the inside pocket. I place it on the table and push it down to her side. "Here it is."

She leans forward and reads the ticket several times to make sure it's legitimate. "Wow."

We sit and stare at the ticket as if it's the Holy Grail. She snaps out of her trance and looks up at me. "Excellent. I have several questions to start the process. Let us begin, shall we?"

She shifts in her seat to make herself more comfortable. In front of her is a pad of paper and a pen, and she appears to be taking notes.

"Have you called the lottery organization yet?"

"No, I haven't."

"That's not a problem. I can help with that step and do that on your behalf. Now, let's talk about the sum. I want to mention that, even though you have won five million dollars, you won't see that total amount, because, as you imagine, you need to pay taxes on it. It's considered income."

I swallow a lump in my throat. "Okay."

"Nothing to be nervous about. You're still going to end up with a large sum of money," she says. "What do you do?"

"I work at a restaurant nearby."

"I see. Are you planning on quitting your job?"

I shrug. "I don't know. Maybe. It depends on how soon they can find someone to replace me." Who am I kidding? I can't wait to tell Barbara I quit.

Sam lets out a small laugh. "That's awfully nice of you. I've heard of people storming into their boss's office as soon as they learn of their winning and giving them a piece of their mind. Bad idea!"

I nod. "I agree." At the same time, I can't help but picture doing that very same thing to Barbara. I don't consider myself a mean person, but it would give me a little satisfaction.

"Winning the lottery can be tricky." She stares at me and continues. "You never know who's going to be after your money."

A chill goes down my spine. There is something in her voice that makes her statement sinister.

"Mind elaborating?"

"Well, don't be surprised if you suddenly hear from your third or fifth cousins you haven't spoken in five million years." She laughs. "Just wait and see."

That won't be an issue. Jimmy and I don't have any close family. We don't even have extended family that I know of, or, if we do, we haven't spoken with them in decades. Our marriage has isolated us from everyone. Maybe it's the reason we've stuck together as long as we have.

"We don't have any family," I offer.

"And who's we? Are you married?"

"Yes. I've been married for almost thirty years."

"Congratulations!" Sam cries. "That's a rarity these days."

If she only knew what those thirty years looked like, she'd think differently. I look at her left hand and don't see a ring. A sliver of jealousy washes over me as I imagine what my life as a single person could be.

"Thanks," I say.

"Now, let's talk about the money. With the taxes taken out, you'd receive around three-and-a half million, give or take. Like I said, since this is still a significant amount, I suggest you find a financial planner to help you with investing it. I have a friend I can refer you to. He is excellent. Would you prefer to take the money as annuity or as a lump sum?"

"Lump sum," I say, giving no thought or hesitation.

"Lump sum. Okay. Most people choose to take it as the annuity, because you end up paying fewer taxes and it's easier to manage. But I let my clients make their ultimate choice, even though I always advise them to go with the annuity option."

"No," I say firmly. "I want the lump sum."

"I see." Sam looks at me as if studying me. "Out of curiosity, why do you prefer the lump sum?"

"I'm planning on giving it all to charity."

Now Sam shifts in her seat and clears her throat. She frowns as she stares at the table in front of her and plays with her fingers.

"I beg your pardon. Did you say you will give it all to charity?"

I nod. "I mean, yes, besides maybe taking a vacation and taking care of some unfinished personal business, which shouldn't cost too much, I'm planning on giving it to charity."

"Have you discussed this with your husband?"

"No." I shake my head. "Should I?"

"I'm afraid, as a married couple, you need to decide together."

"Why? I won the ticket, not him. I can do with my money as I please. He does the same with his. We have separate checking and savings accounts." Both have been nearly empty for a while.

"A decision like this can lead to straining of your marriage and even a divorce."

I would be so darn lucky.

"Now, not as a lawyer, but as a human with feelings

and reasons, I would highly suggest you sleep on your decision."

"No." I shake my head. "I've already made my decision. If you're worried about getting paid, don't be, because that's also part of my plan."

Sam shifts in her chair again and nods her head fast. "Of course, I wasn't worried." She sighs as if shaking off terrible news. She finally turns to me and says, "So, what's your choice of charity? Do you have something in mind already?"

"Maybe. I'm still considering my options," I say.

She tilts her head to the side and narrows her eyes at me. "I'm curious. Is there a story behind all this?"

CHAPTER 6

OF COURSE, there's a story behind all this. And of course, I don't tell Sam anything. My past is none of her business. It's most definitely no one's business. I shrug off her question, shaking my head. "No, there's no story."

I imagine I sound like a lunatic to her, but I will play the game.

She moves on from the question. "I'm going to call the lottery and help redeem the ticket. Do you have your checking account number on you?"

"Ah, yes." I carry it with me all the time even though I've rarely needed it. Jimmy has handled the big purchases for the house in the past, and as of late, no one has.

I give her my checkbook, and she dutifully jots down the information on her pad. She lifts her head and looks at me with her giant, inquisitive eyes.

"Don't be surprised if a lot of media attempts to interview you once the lottery has your information."

"Media?"

"That's right. They will release your name immediately."

Picturing my name all over the news makes me uneasy. "Is there any way to avoid the release of my name? I mean, why do they need to do that?"

"Unfortunately, in the state of New Hampshire, winning the lottery cannot be anonymous."

I want to ask why, but I somehow doubt Sam knows the actual answer.

The door opens up, and Emily comes in. She's carrying a cup of coffee that both Sam and I seem to have forgotten. Emily looks frazzled, and she puts the cup in front of me, gazing at Sam. I can tell she fears her boss, as she trembles when she speaks. "I'm so sorry. It got so busy, and the coffee machine wasn't working properly at first."

Sam waves her hand. "No worries. Thank you, Emily."

Emily looks at me, her brows stitched together in frustration. She looks young, with so much potential, but I wonder if her fear will impede her success.

"Thank you, Emily," I repeat.

We wait for Emily to exit, then Sam continues, "How would you feel appearing on TV?"

I stare at Sam, lost for words.

She smiles. "The lottery organization loves to advertise success stories. And, if I'm frank, people love seeing them. It gives them hope that they, too, can win."

"I've got nothing to lose," I say, even though I'm apprehensive. "As long as I don't need to disclose where the money goes."

"That won't be a problem," Sam says. She stands up and extends her arm. "It's a pleasure doing business with you, Lynn. We will be in touch soon."

I shake her hand and stand up, a little unsure of myself. "If you need anything else, let me know," I say.

"Absolutely," she says. "Oh. Actually, there's one more thing. Where should I send the invoice?"

"The invoice?"

"Yes. For my services."

Of course. The invoice. "I will bring the check in as soon as I get the money. Is that okay?"

I'd love to pay her immediately, but I'm broke as hell. Once the tourist season dies, so does the restaurant business, and I barely make any money between October and May.

"That's fine," she says.

On my way back home, I stop by the restaurant to tell Barbara I'm not feeling well, and that I'm skipping my shift tonight. I can't bring myself to tell her about my win, but she will find out soon enough. Heck, the whole town—the whole *state*—will find out soon enough!

"What's the matter?" she says. Her voice is full of annoyance and aggravation.

"I'm not feeling well, that's all."

"You've got your period?" She laughs, then stops abruptly, probably remembering my age. I'm over fifty, and that train passed long ago.

"I'll see you later, Barbara. Take care."

Leaving the restaurant, my shoulders sag with relief

that I won't have to tolerate Barbara's disrespectful tone or constant nagging anymore. I can't say she' always been this bad--she'd given me this job even after I'd acted like a full-fledged asshole--but sometimes, her tone just gets to me. This is just who Barbara is. A person with pain and suffering of her own.

Jimmy's presence in the house surprises me when I go inside. He isn't working today, either. He's lounging in the recliner, watching TV, a beer in his hand. A bunch of empty bottles sit on the coffee table, and I can't count fast enough how many. His eyes are heavy, darting around the TV set until he looks at me and says, "Where have you been?"

I stand in front of him, contemplating my best answer. He sizes me up and down, curling up his nose at the realization I'm dressed up. His facial expression changes from one of anger to fear, as his eyes bulge at me. He knows the stakes are high, and he clearly doesn't want to lose the chance of a better life.

"I'm asking where you've been."

"I went to see a lawyer," I say. "We're working on the next steps to get the lottery money."

"Why didn't you tell me?"

I shrug. "What difference does it make? You never tell me when you go places."

That statement pisses Jimmy off. He propels himself from the chair and lunges at me. He grabs my hair and pulls me toward the wall, banging my head against it. I can feel the warm blood trickling out, and I extend my arms to steady myself, but I'm feeling blinded. The wall seems too far away. Jimmy releases my hair, and I fall to the ground, immediately reaching for my knees and curling into a ball. The pain is unbearable.

Jimmy walks away and sits back in the recliner, setting his eyes on the TV as if nothing just happened.

He mumbles, "Don't you ever leave the house without telling me where you're going again. Ever."

Tears trickle down my face. But this will be over soon.

Sooner than I want.

CHAPTER 7

THINGS HAVEN'T ALWAYS BEEN this bad with Jimmy. It started on a day I will never forget. The day that allowed Jimmy to behave like a monster.

The memory brings me to the hospital where I wake up in a cold sweat, forgetting where I am. It's the year 1997, but I have no idea what day or month it could be. It's bright outside, albeit cloudy, and all I can see through the window are trees with leaves turning yellow and brown, a sure sign the fall has come. My room is on the second floor, so I see the buildings across the way. I've lost count of the number of days I've been here. I might have been admitted for days, for months, forever.

I'm feeling different. Vacant.

The nurse storms into my room without knocking and greets me with a high-pitch voice. "Good morning."

My eyes dart around the room, following her path. Her energy is palpable, something I couldn't ever match in a million years. She gazes at me and smiles, then she approaches to check my blood pressure. "You're getting out of the hospital today. Your husband is coming to pick you up."

I nod as I draw the covers in. I'm cold even though the room is heated at a decent temperature, and I am wearing layers of clothes—a cotton shirt and hospital scrubs.

I don't ask questions, as I'm still feeling disoriented, but I'm curious to know what has transpired in the past few days. I don't know why, but I fear the answer. I'll find out in time.

As I wait for Jimmy to pick me up, I wonder who's been feeding my baby. No one has woken me up once to feed, and I find it strange. My breasts feel swollen and I don't know what to do with the milk I haven't used or pumped. I run my hands over the clothes and feel the wetness. I've been in a trance-like state, trying to beat the withdrawal, oblivious to my surroundings. I am in the dark, the deep, atrocious dark, the rock bottom, and I don't know how to turn around and get myself out of it.

They've told me I may not sleep at all after giving birth, but in contrast, I've slept too much, almost like I've been in a coma of some kind. They call it a postpartum depression, the inability to grapple with the new reality. While they offer the diagnosis with razor precision, they don't seem to have a solution. Anti-depressant drugs maybe? Though, it's drugs that got me here in the first place, so maybe not the best solution. I hope that Jimmy will have the courage to care for me.

Jimmy arrives in my room an hour later. He grabs me by the arm and lifts me up, as if eager to get out of here. I've changed out of the hospital scrubs and put on the oversized overalls that fit me just right when I first arrived here. There's a vast gap, emptiness, where the belly section is. Jimmy doesn't look me in the eye. He says nothing as he signs the discharge papers. The nurses bid us good luck and tell us they hope to see us again, but something tells me I won't see this hospital unit ever again. We walk through the hospital hallways, a maze of paths leading to the exit. I walk slowly because my crotch is in pain. My feet are swollen. My body is weak and I can't wait to curl up in bed and sleep.

Not until we walk through the door does it occur to me we are walking out empty-handed. Jimmy doesn't offer an explanation, and I don't ask. But I think I understand the implication.

Jimmy is intently focused on the road while driving us home. This beach town has died out and the tourist season is over. It's definitely Fall. There's hardly anyone around anymore. The temperature outside has fallen, and the brisk air is a welcome reprieve from the past hot summer. It was a scorching one. Dragging myself around while carrying the baby in the heat was a hell of an undertaking. Thankfully, the beach is nearby, so I was able to cool myself down next to the ocean.

"What happened?" I finally ask.

I'm afraid to meet his eyes, but in my periphery, I sense Jimmy turning in my direction while holding the wheel in one hand and a lit cigarette in the other. We've told each other we'd quit smoking when the baby comes, but now I wonder if there's any need.

He flicks the cigarette up in the air and grabs the wheel with the freed hand.

"He didn't make it." He's looking straight ahead, showing neither sadness nor remorse for the lack of it.

I bow my head and notice my shaky hands on my lap. "I'm sorry."

I look up at Jimmy, who is staring at me with his menacing eyes. He remains quiet. His silence scares me. I don't know what it means, why he's not responding. I fear the worst, which is that he hasn't forgiven me and never will.

Home is quiet when we get there. There's a mess that Jimmy left behind while I was at the hospital. His clothes are spread on the couch, the living room floor, the bed. A stack of dishes wobbles precariously in the kitchen sink. Leftover food in the Styrofoam cups is taking over the kitchen cabinet tops. Several empty beer bottles sit on the coffee table. Did Jimmy invite guests over, or was it him who was drinking? If it's him, it's new, but I don't dare ask.

The brand-new recliner chair we got for me to nurse in is still sitting in the corner, even though its purpose is no longer there. Jimmy must not have bothered to return it. The arsenal of baby stuff—blankets, pacifiers, bottles, clothes—all in blue, are scattered around the house. Jimmy will need to get rid of them, because I have no strength to put myself to the task. I look around and see the house with indifference, and head for the bed.

That night, Jimmy slept in the living room. He lets me take over the bedroom, where I can hide my new feelings of inadequacy and guilt. In the morning, when I wake up, I feel something or someone hovering over me. As I peel my eyes open, I see it's Jimmy standing next to my bed.

"Get up."

I stare at him wide-eyed, and I can't tell if his intentions are good or bad.

"Get up," he repeats.

"I can't, Jimmy. I just can't."

"Yes, you can, and yes, you will."

I shake my head. "Jimmy... please. Call Skull for me." My eyes are begging him to cave and help me. Just one more time. Until all this mess of my life blows over, and then I will be done for good.

"Who? Skull? Are you crazy?"

Jimmy tears the covers from the top of me and throws them to the floor. I feel the cold air and I get instant goosebumps. He grabs my arm and pulls me toward him. I try to yank my hand, but he's a lot stronger than me. Those biceps of his can do a lot of damage if he used them.

He drags me across the bed, and I fall to the floor, bumping my head. I get into a curled-up position and remain still, hoping Jimmy leaves me alone.

"Do something with your life, for fuck's sake. Go to work, cook dinner, do something!"

His voice is overbearing, and his words sting.

"Call Skull. For me. Please."

Jimmy storms out of the bedroom, and seconds later, I hear the front door slam. I climb into bed. A small strip of light comes through the window, and I put the covers over my head. My eyes are closed shut, and I'm sweating like a pig. The shivers are shaking my whole body in even beats, and all I want is death. The landline phone rings, but I cannot get up and answer. It rings and rings until it halts. The voicemail picks up.

"Lynn? Lynn? Are you there? Pick up, damn it! Lynn!"

I block my ears. The sound from the phone is muffled, and I can't hear the words anymore. The sounds are making me want to throw up, and I hate throwing up. I've done it so many times, my insides hurt.

When Jimmy comes home that evening, I'm still in the same position. I've barely moved. He's yelling out of the living room, "Lynn? Lynn, where the hell are you?"

He sounds angry. It's the first time I've heard Jimmy's voice filled with repulsion, and it sends shivers down my spine. I don't blame him for his reaction, but I'm genuinely scared.

"Lynn, come out of the bedroom! Did you cook dinner today?"

I think he knows the answer, but he is trying to make a point of how useless around the house I have been. He trots over to my bed and rips the cover off me. "Get up, for fuck's sakes."

I roll off the bed and go to the kitchen, feeling lost. Maybe I should make a simple meal, so I can appease

Jimmy, but my body is still recovering and I'm so weak. "I can call Barbara and have food delivered. What do you think?" I plead with Jimmy, hoping he will understand. But he'd clearly rather I prove myself worthy of this marriage.

"You're hopeless." He storms out of the kitchen, a beer in his hand.

My knees buckle beneath me. If Jimmy only knew how much I am craving the fix. But I don't think I can share anything of that nature with him anymore.

"Jimmy." I move to the living room, my arms dangling by my side. "I'm so sorry. Please hear me out. I need help."

Jimmy shakes his head. "No, no. Not that kind of help. Pull yourself together, will you? Enough with the pity party."

I bow my head and slump my shoulders. Jimmy gets on his feet. He has gulped down his beer and heads to the kitchen to get another one. He stops in front of me, and his eyes are filled with disgust. What has happened to Jimmy? He tolerated my drug use before, but now it seems completely off limits. I question whether he ever was happy that I was an addict. Maybe the loss of our son proves that he always hated me for it, but now he finally has a chance, a reason to act out on it.

He violently shakes my shoulders. "You're a damn liar. A witch and a liar!" Then he raises his hand, swings it, and slaps me across my left cheek.

My hand lands on my face involuntarily. My ears are

ringing, and my eyes bulge from the pressure of Jimmy's strike.

I stay calm. Jimmy walks away, and I stand there, feeling the burn on my cheek. And then, something else happens I didn't see coming.

For the first time in many days, months, maybe even years, I strangely feel alive for the very first time.

CHAPTER 8

I'VE HOPED Jimmy will change over years, but still the smallest things set him off, and I pay the price. I didn't think going to see the lawyer would cause him to attack me so violently, but nothing should be a surprise. When I wake up in the morning, I can barely open my eyes. They feel puffy and large. I touch the side of my right eye lightly and shriek in pain.

My bedroom door opens, and it startles me. It's Jimmy. He peaks his head through the door before he comes inside. I draw the cover to my chin as if protecting myself from him. He's the last person I want to see this early in the morning, but I don't say anything, nor do I look at him. Outside, the rain is making a constant commotion while dripping on the open front porch that is yet to be fixed. A single plank is missing and even though it's visible, Jimmy's foot has fallen through so many times when drunk. Everything in this fucking house is falling apart. I used to care a lot more, but now it doesn't matter.

Jimmy is still standing at the door like an unwanted shadow. Sometimes I wonder if the dynamics of our relationship will ever change, or if the change is contingent on our new circumstances. But he is a hothead and I've seen him cause trouble in public many times before. He'd start a fight if he perceived someone's look to be ill-intended, or he would insult a passer-by because they looked different from him.

People have called cops on him multiple times. But he knows almost all the cops in town, his biggest advantage in life, given his personality. In fact, many like to drop their car at the shop for repair, and sometimes for free—so Jimmy has gotten away from a bunch of problems. By now, he has avoided appearing in court or going to jail several times, and as long as he knows he will have that cover, he will act up as badly and as often as he wants to.

I've been suspicious all along, but I also discover that he had made a call to the TV station, attempting to coax Scott into listing his name right alongside mine, as though he were a victor in this as well. Jimmy's knack for cunning maneuvers and his uncanny ability to evade consequences have always left me wondering: How does he manage it?

I often wonder what else he has been getting away with that he's not telling me.

But beatings and insults at home? *Exhale*. Domestic abuse for Jimmy is a walk in a park. A little game he likes to consider a necessity in our marriage. And I surrendered long ago.

"Hey." His voice sounds soft.

With eyes half open, my vision is blurry and I can only see his body contours getting closer.

"What do you want?"

He sits on the edge of the bed and looks at me. I can see him better now, and I convince myself that repentance covers his face.

"Nothin'," he says. "I'm sorry about what I did last night. I got carried away, I swear."

I say nothing. His apology doesn't surprise me. Somehow, it makes me feel like I'm a person he shouldn't reckon with. The only way for him to tap into my wealth is if he maintains a cordial relationship between us. Jimmy is a hothead, but he's not dumb. He knows when it best serves him to behave like a human. Maybe he'll leave me alone for good this time.

He reaches out to touch my face, but I yank my head out of his way. "Don't."

"I won't do it again, I swear."

"Okay."

I avoid Jimmy's eyes, as I can't stand to look at him. The sound of rain is the only thing breaking our awkward silence.

"Are you working today?" I ask.

"Working?" He shifts in the seat and rubs the back of his neck.

I am super annoyed that he's skipped work two days in a row.

"Yeah. Working." I say.

"Maybe I'll stop by for a few hours later. It's usually quiet when it rains."

Jimmy runs excuses whenever convenient. I turn to him and give him the look that makes him jump. He stands up and exits the room. I close my eyes and sigh in relief. On my bedside table, my phone is buzzing. I pick up and see a text message from Samantha:

Hello Lynn, we have claimed your ticket, and we will deposit the money in your checking account within two weeks. My financial advisor friend is expecting your call. Here is his phone number...

It surprises me she didn't call me to deliver such important news. There's something impersonal about getting a text instead of a call. I shake off the thoughts as the renewed energy washes over me when I think of millions hitting my checking account. In two weeks. Holy shit!

Later that day, my phone floods with messages. I've missed several calls from the local phone numbers I don't have saved on my phone or that I recognize. A reporter at the local Hampton news station has left a voice mail, practically begging me to call him back. *We would love you to appear on TV.* He sounds young and enthusiastic, akin to a salesperson.

The entire ordeal has me nervous. I don't know what appearing on TV will do for me. What's everyone going to think? A display of luck? What's Barbara going to say when she realizes I'm about to quit? Is she going to miss me? After almost thirty years of being her employee. I'm practicing my cheerful disposition for TV, but the bathroom mirror says otherwise. The image portrays a broken soul. I lean forward over the sink and turn to the side to inspect the injury inflicted last night. A blue bruise is forming under my eyes, and I am certain it will take a good amount of makeup to conceal it. Jimmy's beating last night comes at the worst time.

Regardless, I pick up my phone and call the news station back to volunteer for the interview.

I want to soak up in all the glory.

I wash my face carefully and tap the towel lightly so not to reopen the wound. When I stand up, I see Jimmy in the mirror, staring at me. He's back from "work", if he ever made it there today. I gasp and turn around quickly.

"What's up?"

"Did you get the money yet?"

"No, not yet. Why do you ask?"

"No reason. I'm just curious." Jimmy is smiling. "When are you gonna get it?"

I think he has something particular in mind, but I don't care to find out.

"My lawyer told me it would take a couple of months." I nod quickly as I speak, trying to stay calm and convincing.

He turns his head to the side and narrows his eyes. A smile lingers on his face, making him look borderline creepy. "Are you lying to me, baby-face?"

I shake my head. "No, no. Why would I lie? It takes that long because it's a large sum of money."

A staring contest commences between us.

"You better tell the truth. You know I don't like when you lie. We've been there." He clicks his tongue and cocks his head. "You remember where the lying gets us?" Jimmy likes to remind me of the old days. He knows well I don't like to remember. Every time he does, guilt oozes out of me. It slides and sticks, and I can't get rid of it.

"I'm about to call the news station. They want me to be on TV."

"Yeah?"

"Yep. Maybe you can come along?"

I don't want him there, but if I offer something he can look forward to, we will repair a little trust that's left, at least temporarily. He forms a smile. "Yeah, I'll come."

"Okay. Let me call the TV station back."

I pick up the phone and dial the TV station and ask for Scott. Jimmy stands and stares at me, wide-eyed. I feel he knows more than he is willing to admit, but I don't dare ask.

CHAPTER 9

THE JOURNALIST at the Hampton news station, Scott, has scheduled our TV appearance for the following day. I don't know what to expect from the experience, but in the past, I've seen other winners appear briefly on the news, a range of emotions on their faces: happiness, bewilderment, surprise... fear. When you suddenly become a millionaire, I suppose a lot of doors in life open up. Some look more welcoming than others, but in general, the world becomes your oyster, and you are a little scared to step inside and explore.

You never know what's on the other side.

Jimmy is up early in the morning. He's in the kitchen, making coffee and whistling. The smell of eggs wafts through the house, leaving me in shock. Is Jimmy cooking? After so many years?

"Hey, Lynn," he screeches. "Do you remember where I left my red tie?"

He looks like a child in a candy store. His face is bright,

and a smile lingers on his face. I don't remember Jimmy ever being cheerful like this. The fragments of our earlier life—more peaceful—are forever clouded by that dreadful event in 1997. Over the years, our marriage morphed into a perpetual cycle of sadness and fear. We haven't laughed or partaken in a fun activity together in so long. Appearing on TV comes closest to it.

I'm lying in bed still, feeling fatigued. I know it's my cancer. No one knows about it, and no one ever will. If I told Jimmy, the first thing he'd force me to do is write up a will and leave all the money to him, which I'm sure he'd spend on expensive cars and booze.

"Lynn?"

"I'll look." My voice is barely above a whisper.

"What?"

I make more effort and raise my voice by a few decibels. "I will look, I said."

I drag myself out of bed and head to the small hallway connecting all the parts of the house. A small closet we rarely open sits between the kitchen and the bedroom. Jimmy has kept some basic house tools and a chainsaw inside, because there's no other place to put all that stuff. We don't have a garage or a basement, and there's no tool shed in the backyard. Jimmy had piled trash in a corner of our small yard covered in weeds, and then he eventually burned it all because he was getting sick of watching it.

I open the closet, surprised that everything is in place. Kneeling down, I get a better view of the bottom shelf. In the shelf's corner, the red material jumps out, and I know this is Jimmy's tie. We've used it for everything but its true purpose. I pull it out, and it's looking rough, as if an animal had chewed it.

"I don't think you want to wear this one." I say, holding it gingerly with just two fingers.

Jimmy materializes in the hallway and looks at the tie. "You just iron it a little and it will look fine."

I don't argue with Jimmy. I never do. The iron is next to the chainsaw, so I take it out and run it over the tie a few times. It still looks like shit, but maybe it won't look so bad on TV, from a fair distance.

When Jimmy sees it, he claps his hands and rubs them together. "Good job, Lynn! Let's do this thing!"

He's in an overly good mood, and I need to stay careful not to tip it over or reveal my plan by accident. I have to be extra cautious of every word I utter from now on. I go back to my room and find a dress for today's occasion. In the bathroom, I apply a copious amount of makeup around my eyes. It conceals the color, but not the shape. The pain is still unbearable, but I've already popped a couple of Ibuprofen. If anyone asks, I'll say I fell down the stairs, even though our house doesn't have any, besides the two leading to the front door. But no one will know.

We eat our breakfast, the burnt eggs and slices of bread, then get ready. Jimmy is wearing a suit he hasn't worn in ages. The legs are too short, and the sleeves are too long. It still fits him perfectly around his torso and abs, as his weight is the same as when he first bought it. He looks at me with pride on his face and says, "How do I look?"

"Good," I say.

"Just good?"

"Great. You look great."

He checks himself out in the bathroom mirror, then turns in my direction, his eyes bulging at me. He doesn't seem so sure of himself now, but he's quiet, and I know better not to rock his confidence.

"Let's go," he says.

The TV station is one town over. The traffic is light at lunchtime. Jimmy drives us, weaving on the road, passing the other cars. We're in no rush, but this is how he usually drives. My body sags with relief when we arrive without having gotten into an accident. Jimmy looks at me as if he wants to say something, but he changes his mind.

It looks like an old building from the outside, but the station is elegantly decorated in the inside. A large front desk sits in the middle of the ground floor, and a young woman stands behind it, staring at us, trying to catch our eyes. I walk up to her gingerly, introduce myself, and tell her we have an appointment. She picks up the phone and talks to someone.

Shortly after, a young man walks out of the corner, wearing a snappy suit and a freshly done haircut. He approaches me, extending his arm, and says, "You must be Lynn."

Jimmy comes near and says, "This is Lynn. I'm James."

The young man doesn't pay attention to Jimmy and says, "I'm Scott. Follow me."

He brings us to a studio in the back where cameras have been set up ready for us. An older man with gray hair with a beard and mustache comes and introduces himself as the president of the lottery organization. He asks a few questions, like where I bought the ticket, what I would do with the money, and I'm careful to say the mantra I've been repeating in my head: Pay off debt, buy a new house, share with friends and family. Scott is standing next to him and taking notes for what he explained would be a brief article on the TV station's website. A photographer has arrived, too, and is standing next to Scott, waiting for an excellent opportunity to take pictures. It makes me feel so important, but suddenly also cheap.

"Please step onto the stage."

I do as they ask, and Jimmy follows me. Someone grabs an enormous sign, resembling a check with my name and five million dollars inscribed on it. With my sweaty palms, I hold it in one corner and Jimmy holds the other.

Someone says, "Smile. We're rolling."

Jimmy doesn't need to be told to smile. As I look straight at the camera, claustrophobia overwhelms me. Everyone is staring at us and a sense of foreboding trickles in. Suddenly, I know this is a bad idea. It's too late to back out. My feet are already on the stage, paralyzed. Maybe I'm just getting paranoid. I talk myself out of the fear and force a bright smile.

CHAPTER 10

THE EXCITEMENT of the moment captured by the news station wanes off as soon as we exit the building.

We ride home in silence. I look out the window at the ocean, contemplating what I've just done. Scott told us we'd appear on the news tonight, but when I picture myself on TV, I feel vulnerable. Have I made a big mistake?

I turn to Jimmy, who looks infuriated. He's clenching the steering wheel hard and looking straight ahead.

"That Scott guy... I wanted to punch him in the face." Jimmy's spittle flies out of his mouth.

I turn to him and see his jaw tightened, his eyes glazed over.

"What did he do to you?" I say, a calmness in my voice.

"He can't just ignore me like that."

I've always thought Jimmy had an inferiority complex, but this brings it to the next level. I also want to remind him that it was me who won the lottery, but I don't want to make the matters worse.

"Don't take it too personal. He probably didn't mean to."

He turns to me with disgust on his face, paying no attention to the road. "Are you with me or with him?"

"I'm with you. I don't know why you're even asking me this question."

"Then don't fucking defend the guy!" Jimmy yells from the top of his lungs and his veins protrude from his neck. The noise deafens me for a second. I resort to silence to avoid provoking him further. I wonder if he would ever chill, even if he were to get the life he wants. I doubt it.

When we arrive home, I notice something sitting on the bottom step at the front door. While still sitting in the car pulled into the driveway, I can't quite tell what it is. It looks like a box. My eyes are etched on the object, anticipating what it might be. Our deliveries are almost non-existent. We don't buy things online, because we are cash people and we buy locally. We only purchase essential items, like groceries, and lately, we've been neglecting even that. Having cancer, my appetite has died out, and I have no desire to eat.

I approach the box and take it in my hands. Not heavy. Jimmy is right behind me, not giving two shits. When we enter the house, I place the box on the coffee table and open it. As soon as I do, a pleasant aroma hits me and the image of the most beautiful flowers—daisies, roses, daffodils—puts a smile on my face. I pick up the note sitting on the top of the bouquet and read: CONGRATULATIONS. It's a lovely gesture, but it seems rather peculiar that there's no signature or name attached to it.

I turn to Jimmy and narrow my eyes. "Did you buy me these flowers?"

Jimmy's pointing the remote at the TV. He turns around to look at the flowers before turning back to the screen. "Nope."

"Then who did it?" It's a rhetorical question I don't expect an answer to, but my mind shifts into the fear mode and speculates. After wracking my brain, I still can't think of anyone. The news isn't out yet, and the only people who know I won the lottery are Jimmy and my lawyer, Samantha.

"Must be your secret admirer." Jimmy looks at me with a smirk.

The way he says it brings chills to my spine. I take my phone and dial the flower shop listed on the label at the top of the box. A man answers the phone after two rings. I introduce myself and inquire about the secret delivery at my house. "Can you tell me who it came from?" The silence on the other line sends me bad vibes. "I'm sorry, but I can't give you the information because of our customers' confidentiality. I simply can't disclose it. Sorry."

"But this could be serious. Please, sir. I need to know the name."

He apologizes again and hangs up on me.

"Great," I whisper.

Next, I text Sam, my lawyer. She is the only other

person who knows about the winning. "Should I thank you for the flowers?"

I put the phone next to me as I sit on the couch and stare at it, anticipating her response. After ten minutes, my phone buzzes. And it's Sam: *What flowers?*

Shit.

I consider the possibility that the TV station or the lottery organization might have done it, but wouldn't they just hand it to me in person less than an hour ago? That seems more logical. I call the TV station, just in case, and get a similar answer to Sam's. No one who knows I won the lottery seems to be the sender.

For the rest of the day, I try not to think about the mystery sender, even though it spooks me. I only hope that someone's not after me, like Sam might have suggested. Jimmy and I sit in front of the TV and wait for the news. Scott told us our appearance would be on the five and six-thirty news. We don't want to miss it. Jimmy is on a daydreaming kick again about all the things we'll buy soon.

"I saw a sales sign in front of a house on the hill. We can buy it with cash."

I grunt. "Yeah, okay."

"I was thinking, maybe we can call David," Jimmy quips.

"Who's David?"

"You know the guy from HGTV doing that show, *My Lottery Dream Home*." Jimmy laughs. My eyes do a major roll. "No mortgage for the rest of your life. How's that sound?"

"Sounds good," I sound agreeable, but not too committal. Whatever Jimmy wants to buy, I'll say I want to buy. Because why not? We have a lot of money, and it's all a lie, anyway.

"We can invest the rest and live off of it for the rest of the life. You hear what I'm sayin'?"

"Yes. But Barbara won't like it. She can't find any people to work for her to save her life."

"Fuck Barbara. She's trouble. That woman is trouble. You don't owe her nothing. Stop feeling guilty."

That's funny hearing from Jimmy. He knows guilt is all I've felt all these years, for a different reason. It's not like you can just shake off guilt and live happily ever after. Years of therapy could help to teach you how to cope, but even then... this kind of guilt is permanently attached to my soul.

Jimmy hates Barbara. It's she who got me started on drugs. One night, she asked me to stay an extra shift, because another waiter was sick and couldn't make it. I told her I was exhausted and would rather head back home, but she gave me a charming look and told me to follow her. I walked behind her to the bathroom, and she entered the handicap stall, asking me to join her. Hesitant, I did what she asked me to do, because I was afraid I would lose my job if I didn't. And I couldn't afford to lose my job. It was too late now to go back and finish high school.

"Close the door," she'd said.

I closed the door behind, and Barbara took something out of her pocket. She put white powder on her hand and instructed me to snort it. At first, I didn't want to, but I'm the kind of person who wants to prove I'm capable of anything I put my myself to, so I leaned down and snorted it. I felt an instant rush of energy. I was on top of the world.

I was hooked.

I snap out of my thoughts when Jimmy puts the TV volume up high. "Here we go."

The breaking news goes first. We stare at the TV in silence, waiting to see our faces shining out from the screen. I can't concentrate on what's being shown. The flowers on the coffee table serve as a constant reminder that someone out there knows more about me than I'm willing to acknowledge. But who? Sweat beads down my neck and my hands are clammy. That someone else knows who I am or where I am makes my stomach churn. All these years, no one has wanted to be near us. No one wants to be associated with a tragedy, the death in our eyes, the sullen looks on our faces. People run away from us as far as possible.

Ten minutes in, we can see ourselves standing on the stage, holding the large five-million-dollar fake check. Jimmy is glowing, while I'm staring at the camera, fear projecting from my eyes.

"Look at us, Lynn, look!"

I look more closely, and the image of myself startles me.

I start to feel surer than ever that I've made a terrible mistake.

CHAPTER 11

JIMMY LETS out a heartfelt laugh when he sees us on TV. He gets up and goes to the fridge to fetch himself a beer. I'm not in the mood for him to get drunk and provoked and violent tonight. I go to the bedroom for some quiet.

"Where are you going?" He's holding the fridge door as he watches me trot to the bedroom. "Don't you wanna celebrate?"

"Sorry, not tonight. It's been a long day already." These days I get exhausted easily, but I don't tell him that. It's been an emotional rollercoaster ride the past couple of days.

He turns to look at the fridge and says nothing to comfort me. Jimmy hasn't once been a source of sympathy ever since the day everything fell apart.

I lie on the bed and close my eyes, fighting the urge to cough hard. I make my face like a blowfish and place my hand on my mouth. It hardly works, but I'd try anything to avoid questions from Jimmy. He needs to keep thinking everything is going as planned. If he knew I was dying, there is no doubt he'd interrogate me about the money and demand I leave a will.

I have no desire to use the remaining time of my life doing that.

My phone buzzes and I pick it up to see who it is. It's a text from an unknown number:

Hey Lynn, it's your cousin Rob. I just saw you on the news. Congratulations. Let's catch up soon.

Oh, cousin Rob! Haven't talked to him in ages. I smile, remembering Sam's words about people from my life reemerging from thin air. I open up the message and delete it without responding. "Fuck off, Rob," I whisper.

Just as I delete his message, my phone buzzes, and I stifle a gasp when I see it's a message from Greta. I haven't talked to her in ages, and thought I had lost her. She's not only seen me on the news, but she also wants to get together soon and catch up. I respond immediately: *Yes, I would love to.*

I drift to sleep, grateful that Jimmy has left me alone tonight.

In the morning, the news is all over the town. Not only do we appear on TV, but we're also plastered all over social media.

Lynn Miller and James Corrigan win big!

I open the Facebook app on my phone on rare occasions, just to check out the funny memes and reels. Babies seem to be the theme of my reels, and I don't know how that came about.

Today is different. Curiosity pulls me in, and I open up the app to check out the comments under the article and see that it has been liked more than a hundred times. Shared over fifty times. We've obviously gained popularity. I click on the article to read the comments. They are mainly positive until I get to the nasty one: I hope these scumbags will share.

It makes me flinch. I click on the person, but their profile picture is the USA flag. It's private, so nothing shows up on their news feed. I'm shaking. This is all far too risky and wild. I'm surprised Jimmy's name makes the news.

I'm sitting on the couch when a knock on the front door brings my attention into full focus. Jimmy is in the bathroom, and I jump at the sound.

I inch towards the door and look through the peephole. It's our next-door neighbor, Rose. A lady in her late sixties who likes to take turns visiting neighboring houses and snooping around. She'd lost her husband when she was young and never cared to remarry. She'd described him as her soul mate, and said no one would ever come close.

I roll my eyes when I see her because I know why she's here. Even though she annoys me, I'm fully aware she's harmless. We've known Rose ever since we moved into this house. With each passing year, to abate loneliness, Rose tends to her garden and treats it like her sanctuary, spending a whole lot of time there while observing the neighbors and passing judgement. She's turned her front yard into a botanic garden, busting with fresh flowers and bushes. I imagine she wanted to share it with someone special, but she could never replace her husband or find someone new she'd care about.

I open the door and greet her in a somber voice. "Hey, Rose."

As soon as she sees me, her face brightens, and she says, "Well, congratulations, dear. I saw you on the news last night."

I haven't seen Rose for months, even though we live next door, but now I can see she has aged. Her face is covered in wrinkles and she speaks slowly, enunciating her words. I don't ask to come in, but she makes the steps toward the door and walks by me, making herself at home. She moves fast for an old lady, even though she has a hump on her back, which doesn't seem to slow her down.

She sits in the recliner and makes herself comfortable. "Isn't that exciting?"

"It is."

"How lucky. What are you going to do with all this money, Lynn?" She keeps her mouth wide open, and I can sense jealousy in her voice and eyes. "You're not going to move out of this house, are you?"

Before I can say anything, she continues, "I don't blame you, dear. You deserve a better life." Her voice sounds pitiful, and I wonder if she knows Jimmy beats me often. She must, surely. But I don't care about her pity.

"We haven't decided yet."

Just as I say this, Jimmy emerges from the corner. "Hey, Rose." His voice is too cheerful for this time of the morning, but this is the new Jimmy I'm still getting used to.

"Hi, dear," Rose says, extending her arms, as if expecting a hug.

Jimmy comes over and gives her a small hug and a kiss on her temple. "I was just asking your wife if you're moving out of this house."

Jimmy smiles and nods. "You better believe it. We're getting out of this shithole, Rose. No offense to you or anyone else living in this row. You can come visit and stay with us anytime."

"Oh, that would be lovely."

They both gaze at me, as if expecting me to say something, but I remain silent. I put my head down, avoiding their eyes.

"Right, Lynn?" Jimmy says.

I look at Rose. "Of course, you can stay with us anytime." I offer a smile to reassure her my offer is genuine.

"You're going to be a celebrity in town. Everyone's already talking about it," Rose says, but then her eyes glaze over with a mysterious look. "But you know, you should be very careful."

Rose stares at me with intense eyes, then whispers, "Lynn, did you hear what I said?" then she lowers her voice even more. "You need to be very careful."

CHAPTER 12

ALL THESE YEARS, Greta has lived one town over. That our paths haven't crossed all these years is a pure miracle. Her life must have taken a different direction than mine. I still remember her being witty and flamboyant while we were in high school. Like me, she didn't like to study hard or turn in her homework on time, but her personality made up for it. She was the magnet to other girls who were desperate to make friends with her. The boys in our classroom gravitated toward her because she didn't care for them much. And boys liked the hunt. The challenge. I'd been the quiet one, happy to have Greta by my side, while she had me and many others. She married a guy ten years older, an upper-middle class guy she met at the beach. I presume she's still happily married, but who the fuck knows? The flamboyant type can also be unpredictable and flaky.

We decide to meet at Pinocchio, a popular Italian restaurant that's been there for decades. As I drive, nerves flutter in my belly at the prospect of encountering a friend who I'd once have given my right arm for. All these years, I've felt ashamed that Jimmy had ruined her wedding, and I couldn't face her. Maybe that was a sign for me to reconsider my marriage, yet I still stood by Jimmy's side.

When I told him I was going to see her, he'd fallen silent. I'm pretty sure he remembers what he did.

When I arrive at the restaurant, I barely recognize her. I'm so startled by her looks that part of me wants to turn around and run. Greta is my age, but she already sports wrinkles all over her body. Her hair is gray, and her eyes have dark and heavy circles.

When she sees me, she stands up from her chair and runs to give me a hug. "Lynn!"

Her smile is radiant, which suddenly shaves off a few years.

"Greta!" I pretend to be happy to see her and conceal my surprise.

"You look great," she says. "You haven't changed a bit... Well, except you seem to have lost a lot of weight."

She places me at arm's length, looks at me up and down, then brings me closer to her and gives me another hug. A tighter and longer one this time. It's been a while since I've felt someone's affection. I don't remember the last time someone hugged me or offered me a kind word. Instead of hugging Greta back, I remain anchored to the spot, with arms by my sides. She lets go of me and takes my hand to lead me to the table.

We sit down. Her smile lingers. "How good to see you, my friend."

She's kind, and I wonder if this is truly genuine or if it has something to do with my sudden wealth. After Jimmy ruined her wedding, I don't see how he, and me by extension, could ever be forgiven.

"It's great to see you, too," I say.

"I... I don't even know where to begin," she says. "I turned on the TV yesterday... I mean, I barely ever watch the news, and there you were. Well, I first saw Jimmy, and I was like, wow, I think I know this guy. But then I looked closer, and I saw you holding the other corner of the check. I was like, hey that's my friend Lynn. You should have heard me screaming."

She offers a heartfelt laugh, and I smile.

"Yeah, so I guess I won the lottery."

"Congratulations."

I nod. "Thank you. It's been quite a ride."

"I guess I don't need to ask you, but it seems you're still married to Jimmy?"

"Um-hm." I nod again and lower my head.

"You know, it's fine. I have forgiven him. It's been so long; I don't even remember what exactly happened." I do. Every minute.

"Thank you. I'll be sure to tell him."

She leans on the seat and looks at me with a smile. "Oh, Lynn. I've really missed you, my friend. I tried to get in touch with you after the wedding, but you never responded to my calls. After a dozen times, I gave up. I wish you'd contacted me."

"I know. I'm sorry. I truly am sorry."

"But we're here again, with so much catching up to do." Greta doesn't skip a beat.

"I suppose." I fear she will notice that my enthusiasm does not match hers in the slightest. Now I'm ashamed to admit that I could have lived without seeing Greta. "Are you still married to ... was it Greg?"

"Great memory!" She laughs. "No. Greg and I divorced a couple of years after we married."

A sudden pit forms in my stomach. I wonder if Jimmy was one reason for their divorce. He put a strain on that marriage on day one. Jimmy and I: are we just two shitty people sharing this planet with those who better deserve it?

"Really?" My brows stitch in distress.

"Yeah, he ended up cheating on me with his ex. Douchebag. But now I'm married to a wonderful man who grew up a couple of blocks from our house. Gerry." She laughs. "I can't get away from G."

The waitress breaks the awkwardness of the moment and asks us to order. When she leaves the table, Greta continues, "So, let me tell you. I've been super busy trying to grow my business the past two years. My husband and I have an insurance company now, but we didn't know how competitive the market is ..."

While she's speaking, I notice a woman in the restaurant's corner staring at me. I don't think I would have noticed her if her stare didn't bore into me with a sense of retribution. I try to avoid her gaze by focusing on Greta, but it's difficult. Her eyes don't leave me, and she's insistent on giving me the penetrating look. She has long black hair, parted in the middle, gigantic eyes and tattoos on her arms. I catch her gaze for a split second and, out of fear, I divert my eyes to Greta. She is talking about God knows what, and I can't concentrate. All I can sense is that she has lived a happy and decent life. I turn my gaze back to the intruder. She's still looking at me. Her face expression is serious. She looks young but fierce. Anxiety washes over me. I ignore her and turn to Greta, looking bewildered. "Lynn, did you hear me?" Greta says. "Do you have any children?"

I jump out of my chair and announce, "I gotta go."

"Lynn?" Greta yells after me. "Lynn, wait!"

I quicken my steps, so she has no chance to catch up to me. I enter my car, turn the engine on, and step on the gas pedal, causing my tires to screech. As I turn the corner, a violent cough catches me off guard. I can barely focus on the road, as my body is violently heaving. I pull onto the shoulder of the road, open the door, and crawl on my knees to the grassy part. When I open my mouth, the blood clots that come out look larger and scarier. I wipe my mouth with my hand and place my head on the ground, closing my eyes.

A sudden honk of the car behind me startles me. "Hey, lady, are you okay? You need help?"

A middle-age man is sitting in his car on the street and looking at me through the open window slot.

My stomach lurches. "Leave me alone!" I scream.

"I'm just trying to help. Geez." He drives away, leaving me kneeling down with my hair disheveled, my body weakened.

What's happening? An indescribable fear and discomfort over everything that's happened the past few days envelopes me, and I'm becoming more distrustful of people. *Is this normal?*

When I arrive home, I pull over in the driveway and smirk when I notice Jimmy's car is there. He must be at home, skipping work again. I wonder if he's already quit his job and moved onto his metaphorical dream life.

Just as I turn the engine off, my eyes catch an object sitting on the top step. My blood freezes. I lean forward at the wheel to get a better look, and I think I see a small box. What is it now? If I were to guess, it's not flowers this time.

I gingerly come out of my car, fearing what the box might contain. The box is black, and the size of a chocolate bar. I pick it up and shake it, but there's not much movement inside. The box is light, and I can't even guess what it is.

Slowly, I pull the side of the box. It's stiff, and it takes me a while to inch it open, revealing its contents gradually.

Then my insides plummet and my eyes widen as they finally work out what it is.

From the top of my lungs, I scream.

CHAPTER 13

JIMMY COMES out of the house, rubbing his eye. "What the hell is going on?"

"Look! Look!" My face is frozen in terror.

"What is it?"

"Look." I hand him the box, and he peers inside.

"What's this?"

"Can't you see? It's a voodoo doll. Someone is after me."

Jimmy's face remains blank, impassive, and he turns around and goes inside the house. I check my surroundings for the culprit, but I don't see anything or anybody suspicious. A few people are walking by, but they're not paying any attention to me. God knows how long this box was sitting on our front steps. I follow Jimmy inside, and he puts the doll on the coffee table. He lies on the couch and puts his arm up to his forehead.

"So, what?" he says.

"What do you mean, so what? Someone is after me.

After the money, Jimmy." I stare at Jimmy from the middle of the living room, my brain searching desperately for answers. "Weren't you here when someone came by? Didn't you hear the front gate door open, for Christ's sake?"

"No. I was busy doing things."

I don't ask what he might be busy with. Jimmy does nothing around the house anymore.

"You don't seem concerned at all, do you?" I scoff. "Don't you see I'm totally fucked here? Someone is after me, Jimmy!"

Jimmy rolls his eyes. "You're just being paranoid. It's probably kids in the neighborhood playing with you."

"Are you shitting me right now? Do you think kids know what a voodoo doll is?"

Jimmy gives me a blank stare and I realize he doesn't know what a voodoo doll is, either.

"Never mind. I'm calling the police."

"Don't be crazy. They won't be able to trace it to anyone. You're just going to waste your precious time."

"It's a threat." My voice shakes as I force the words out. "I'm calling the police."

"Suit yourself. You won't get far—same as the last time you called them," he quips.

I flinch. Last time I called them was a long time ago. It was when Jimmy threatened to kill me one night when he came home drunk. He'd just discovered that I'd be looking for an apartment to live in alone. He'd found a lease application on top of the fridge after I'd accidentally left it lying around. His fury was so intense that no prior beatings matched it. When I called the police, they told me there was nothing to press charges against. It was a verbal dispute, and they don't charge people against insults and foul words. The cop suggested we go to therapy. He was probably one of Jimmy's cop friends.

"But this is different. There's someone out there, watching and following me. The news is out, Jimmy."

"Don't be silly. What exactly do you expect them to do? Hold you hostage? Steal your money?" Jimmy laughs. He sounds so nonchalant, and it's driving me bonkers.

"Yes. Yes. And worse yet, they could kill me."

He waves his hand dismissively and repeats, "Don't be crazy. Just because you've got cash doesn't mean they're after you. It's not like you're the only one around here with money."

I grunt and run to the bedroom, slamming the door behind. I look for my phone, my head yanking left and right, as if lost. My phone is where it always is, in my pocket. My hands shake as I try to unlock it, my slippery fingers fumbling at the keys. I enter the password, but the screen shakes a little, showing the password is incorrect. I repeat the task, slowly and deliberately, until the phone is open.

"Thank God," I whisper.

I dial 9-1-1 and wait for my call to be answered.

"What's your emergency?"

"Hi," I whisper. "I think I'm in trouble." I'm whimpering and doing my best to hold back tears.

"What kind of trouble, ma'am?"

"I think someone is stalking me. I just won the lottery and I think they're after me now."

"Are you injured or hurt, ma'am?"

"No. No." I check myself out automatically. No injury except for a mental one.

"So, what's your emergency?" the woman sounds confused.

"I want the police to investigate this case." I look around the room, fear projecting from my eyes. "Someone sent me flowers yesterday and a voodoo doll today. I don't think I'm safe."

"Ma'am, calm down, please. Can you tell me if you have any clue where these objects come from?"

"No!" I try not to scream, but it's really difficult not to. The urgency of the threat is palpable, and the fear rises inside me like an unstoppable tide.

"Have you received any threatening emails, messages, or photos?"

"No."

"Is there any other evidence you can present to suggest that you're being stalked?"

I pause, feeling defeated. "No."

The woman on the other side of the line gives a quick sigh and continues, "I'm afraid there's not much we can do with this information. If you think this '*stalking*' continues and escalates, call the police right away and we will investigate."

She hangs up on me without giving me any specific

instructions or details on how to spot my stalker. I frown at that thought and throw myself on the bed, staring at the ceiling. Jimmy's voice distracts me when he talks with someone on the phone. I can hear everything he says, even though the bedroom door is closed. He's laughing and talking about having some gigantic party. What party? We barely know anyone anymore.

Then a scary thought crosses my mind. Jimmy might have something to do with this. I cringe as I think of this possibility. He was too quick to dismiss my fear, though to be honest, Jimmy doesn't ever really care about my feelings in general. But there was something sinister in the way he tried to convince me that no one was after me. I shake my head slightly to dislodge the feeling and close my eyes. Could it be someone I might have hurt in the past? After all these years, maybe they are after me.

I keep my eyes closed and make a mental list. Then I start working through it, one by one.

CHAPTER 14

I'M LYING IN BED, doing my best to tune out Jimmy's voice which is projecting throughout the house. He is still yapping on the phone, sounding ecstatic. The rain taps lightly outside, providing a soothing rhythm to accompany my contemplations. With my eyes closed, I wrack my brain for all the people I might have had crossed wires with in the past. I start from my formative years, when I was still maturing and still had a lot to learn.

The list of people I've encountered throughout my life scroll through my mind like a slideshow, each face accompanying by a memory, a fleeting moment. My paranoia fuels wild theories—old classmates, disgruntled coworkers, forgotten acquaintances seeking revenge, all come to mind. But no one in particular comes out as the winner. Everything I've ever done comes down to small quibbles, arguments that came and went and easily forgotten. All my life, I've kept to myself and have done my best not to inflict any kind of pain on humans.

And there were my parents. Now that I'm a grown-up, I can say with all my heart they were decent human beings. They did their best to build a future for me. I grew up with modest means, like many other average American teenagers. Posters of my favorite bands plastered on the walls of my room, listening to music loudly through my Walkman, chasing boys, coming home after the curfew ... maintaining the image of a cool teenager.

I can't say I was the easiest child. Stubborn and rebellious, I couldn't care less about my mother's advice, especially during my blooming years. *Don't have sex before you get married, be careful who you trust, don't do drugs. Don't do drugs. They are evil and they will fuck you up.* Not that she used those words, but she might have as well. Because that's what they did to my life.

My parents are resting in peace now. Not that they would ever come after me. But in my mind, their deaths still haunt me.

My fingers tap against my temple, a subconscious rhythm that matches the rapid beat of my heart. Then, as if by some sinister design, a name emerges from the shadows of my thoughts: Jimmy. My husband.

The realization hits me like a sledgehammer. Jimmy, the one person I have hurt the most, the one whose pain I have tried to bury deep within me. I think back to the arguments, the nights of silence, the tears that have stained our marriage. The constant pursuit of my selfish needs, the late nights at the casino, the gradual distance that has grown between us.

As I lie in bed, staring at the ceiling, I can't escape the crushing weight of guilt settled upon me. The lottery win is supposed to be a chance for me to make amends, to mend what I've broken. But perhaps it's too late. The anonymous gifts are like whispers from the universe, forcing me to confront the consequences of my actions.

As I close my eyes, the darkness of the room envelops me, cocooning me in my own thoughts. The anonymous congratulatory note still lies on the bedside table, a stark reminder that the shadows of doubt have taken root in my mind. But I am determined to unearth the truth, even if it means confronting the darkest corners of my soul.

It pains me to realize that all roads lead to only one person I might have harmed in the past.

And that's Jimmy.

CHAPTER 15

MEMORIES of my marriage drifting away are still fresh in my mind. It's not something I can shake off easily. They linger alongside the guilt, like best friends forever. Like that particular day I was home alone. The bedroom is in disarray. I'm lying on the floor, fighting the urge not to pee myself. With all my strength, I prop myself up and crawl to the bathroom. I take the doorknob and push myself up, somehow getting to the toilet seat. I'm too cold and I can't stop shivering even though the heat is turned on high.

The front door opens, and a voice travels through the house. It's comforting and teases a small smile out of me. I wait for Jimmy to find me. It won't take long. Our studio apartment is small, and I'm sure he can see my feet showing. He walks into the bathroom, puts my arm around his neck, and picks me up. He walks me to the bed and leaves me there and turns around while my eyes follow him. I don't want him to leave, but my mouth is too dry, and I can't utter a word.

Seconds later, Jimmy comes to the bedroom, holding treasure in his hands. I hear a sigh coming out of him, and then the steps approaching the bed.

"Hey. Baby face," he whispers. "I got it."

He sits on the bed beside me, takes my head and puts it on his lap. He caresses my hair and wipes the sweat off my forehead.

"Are you late for your shift again?"

I want to nod, but I'm exhausted. Every muscle, every bone in my body hurts. My lower lip quivers and although I want to tell him it's not by choice, I remain tongue-tied.

"Hey, can you get up?"

I struggle to prop myself up. Jimmy takes me under the armpits, pulls me up, and places my back against the wall. He takes the needle out and fills it with the gold. He gently takes my arm and puts it on his knee. All I feel is heaviness of it, but I know relief is coming.

Jimmy puts the rubber band around my arm and flaps it a few times. It's so tight, the tips of my fingers tingle. Jimmy flaps my arm a couple of more times, and in the corner of my eye, I see the vein protruding, ready for the needle to come through. Jimmy pokes it slowly, then releases all the contents from the syringe. A rush of calmness travels through my body. My eyes roll in my sockets. I slide down the wall and lie on my back, extending my arms out for a hug. Jimmy comes closer and kisses me on the lips.

I pull him in and kiss him back. Then we take our clothes off and make love.

Jimmy pulls a cigarette out of the pack and lights it. "Can I have one?"

He hands me the lit one and repeats the same. We stay in bed, covered in a cloud of smoke. I wriggle closer to Jimmy and put my head on his shoulder. My index finger goes over his tight abs, and he giggles.

We are playful. Jimmy is fun to be around. I love when I make him laugh.

"Do you remember the day we met?" I ask dreamily.

It was only a couple of years ago, when Jimmy first came to the restaurant and set his eyes on me. He'd asked Barbara what my name was and waited for me in the parking lot to come out after my shift. I was just walking to my car when his voice behind startled me. I thought he was going to attack me, but the smile on his face said otherwise.

"I didn't mean to scare you," he'd said.

"Well, you did."

"I'm sorry. Barbara told me you were Lynn. I wanted to introduce myself and say I'd like to get to know you."

I gave him a sideway look, unsure if he was telling the truth. "Why?"

His head snapped and his eyes had bulged, "Whoa, whoa. Little defensive, aren't we?"

"I don't know you, and I don't know what you want."

"Just to take you out for a coffee, maybe? Get to know you?"

We're laughing as we recall the memories.

"I really liked your cheek dimples when you smiled." Jimmy says.

The day after he'd cornered me in the parking lot, Jimmy took me out for a walk by the beach and we spent a few hours talking and getting to know each other. We both seemed to share a similar fate: single children, dead parents. I told him I'd lost my parents recently. My mother died of cancer, and my father had died shortly after her. A broken heart, as they say. I'd heard of couples dying within weeks of each other, but never in a million years did I think this would happen to my parents. I'd just turned eighteen and was barely ready to enter the adult world, but I managed somehow.

Jimmy's story about his parents was different. He didn't want to talk about it. He only mentioned they were no longer in touch. I could surmise that they'd disowned him, or the other way around, but the reasons remained a secret.

Because I felt so lonely, Jimmy was the closest person in my life at the time I met him. He served as a welcome reprieve from the nightmares I was plagued by. When we first started dating and sleeping in the same bed, those nightmares disappeared, and I felt safe. I didn't want to dig into his past. His presence was enough.

The phone rings, pulling Jimmy and me out of our reminiscing. We both stay on bed, wrapped up together as the voicemail picks up, and shortly after, Greta's voice projects through the apartment.

"Lynn? Lynn? It's Great. Please call me. I have some news to tell you. Love you."

Jimmy turns to me and says, "Who's Greta?"

"She's my friend." I say. "You'll get to meet her real soon."

Jimmy looks me up and down and sulks, as if I've just delivered bad news. I give him a little nudge with my fist and laugh. "Hey, don't worry. She's cool. You're gonna like her."

But Jimmy keeps his eyes on one spot. His mood darkens, and he draws silent.

His new dissonance confuses me. I wonder what I've done to disturb our harmony.

CHAPTER 16

PARANOIA REELS me in and doesn't let go. While I'm pretty sure I have a reason to worry, part of me wants to believe I'm just overreacting. Winning the lottery isn't a frequent occurrence; it takes some adjusting and some time to mentally process all of it.

After spending hours and hours ruminating and being sucked deeper into despair, I cave in and call my old therapist, the one I'd been led to by the professionals when dealing with my postpartum depression and a slew of other mental health issues after I'd given birth. She might offer some answers to my questions. Like, why am I feeling this way? I can barely even recognize myself. Or, why does winning the lottery seem to have the opposite effect on me? I should be more peaceful now that I have a chance of redemption, but I'm unsettled and miserable, and all because someone has been stalking me. It's completely rattled me, knocking me out of balance. Maybe there's more at play that I am not realizing. I need Dr. Walker to help me find the answer.

The phone rings, and my body becomes a bundle of nerves. Will Dr. Walker remember me? A young woman answers the phone and asks how she can help. I take that question literally and sprint through a list in my head. Then she speaks again, and her voice brings me back to the present. "Hello?"

I introduce myself as an old patient of Dr. Walker's and explain I'd like to see her again about "a different matter" this time. The young woman asks me if I could elaborate, but I tell her it's complicated. I'd rather do it in person with Dr. Walker. As luck has it, she has an opening tomorrow at eleven in the morning, and I feel a dash of hope that relief is coming. Plus, Jimmy will be at work so I won't need to clear my whereabouts with him.

Tomorrow comes, and I'm ready to face Dr. Walker. On my way to her office I picture what this session might look like twenty-five years later. She'll probably have a laugh inside when I tell her the reasons I want to see her. Still, I remind myself it's good to have someone to talk to, someone who can validate my feelings, whether they are visceral.

Jimmy goes to work today, despite his efforts to stay home and do nothing. Before he slams the exit door, he grunts and cusses.

Dr. Walker's office is in the same old building two towns over. The front office looks the same, except they've painted the walls a different color, and the furniture in the foyer is newer. I remember every detail of her office—I remember staring blankly at those walls, wondering if my life was worth continuing. I remember sitting in the waiting room, in a chair with metal legs and an uncomfortable backrest. All those therapy sessions still didn't bring my guilt to a manageable level. Dr. Walker probably considered me a hopeless case, and she'd encouraged me to continue my healing journey, but what was the point? I was just throwing money on co-payments, the money that I could use for tough days, when Jimmy unleashed his fury and refused to pay rent.

A woman named Gretchen used to work at the front desk and she'd always asked about my well-being before every session. But now it's a younger woman who couldn't care less whether I'm coming or going. I check in and she asks me to sit down and wait.

I twiddle my thumbs while waiting for Dr. Walker to come out and call me. I pick up a magazine from the coffee table, an old edition from a couple of years ago. My mind races and I can't focus on what's in front of me. I put it back on the table and pull my phone out. Before I open up the Facebook app, the office door opens, and Dr. Walker peers through the door.

"Lynn." She's now standing at the door, looking like the old gray-haired lady that she is. She has reduced in size and even though it looks like these twenty five plus years have served her well, she couldn't escape aging. I'm nearly breathless when I see her. I open my mouth, but no words come out.

"Lynn," she says again. "Come on in."

A range of emotions hits me, but mainly embarrassment. All these years, I haven't fixed my life for the better. All those years have passed since Dr. Walker attempted to show me how to cope with my guilt, but I'm apparently not the quickest student in the lessons of life. My life has been as stale as an old piece of bread, and now it's crumbling into pieces.

I walk through the door and find myself in the familiar space where I'd spent hours and hours trying to undo the remnants of terror I'd created. I'm grateful that Dr. Walker had always shown sympathy and never seemed to judge me, even in passing.

"Have a seat." She points at a large comfortable chair in the room's corner. "Pleasure to see you again. It's been a while."

"It has been. Way too long," I say.

"How have you been?"

"Okay."

She tilts her head and stitches her brows in sympathy. "Just okay?"

"Yeah. Well, I'm still ruminating over what happened." I bow my head to avoid her gaze. I want to keep going, but silence suits me better.

"That's normal. There are things in life we never recover from. We just learn to cope." She nods gently, then tilts her head to the other side.

If coping with past guilt involves being beaten by a husband, then I can say I have achieved success.

I'm dying to ask Dr. Walker how she's been and what she's done with her life the past few decades, but it strikes me as inappropriate. Judging from her demeanor and serene nature, she has done a lot better than me.

We sit in silence for a minute until Dr. Walker gets to the point. "So, what can I do for you today, Lynn? What troubles you?"

I take a big breath. No point keeping those words in longer. "I think someone's after me. I've been sent some strange notes after I won the lottery and appeared on TV and social media."

Dr. Walker remains expressionless, even when I mention the lottery, and it's refreshing to see. I continue, "After a couple of days, I received flowers from an unknown sender, and then a voodoo doll, yet a couple of days later."

"A voodoo doll?"

"Yes. Jimmy—"

Dr. Walker raises eyebrows at those words. She looks surprised to hear his name.

"Jimmy thinks it's just the neighbors' kids, but I can't help but think someone is deliberately after me."

"I understand your concerns," Dr. Walker says. "Did you call the police after these threats took place?"

"I did. But I didn't seem to have a strong enough case, so they hung up on me," I say. "I know our neighborhood is relatively safe, so I wonder if I'm just being paranoid, you know. That's why I'm here today. To put my mind at ease and talk things through."

"How much money are we talking about?"

"Five million."

Dr. Walker nods. "I see. That's a lot of money, and there's a reason I am asking. Different people experience different emotions after winning sizeable sums of money. Some feel depressed, and others become more energized and hopeful. In your case, it is possible that the sudden fortune has manifested itself in paranoia."

She spends several minutes explaining the definition of paranoia, and I think it fits the bill. *Suspicion or mistrust of people or their actions without evidence or justification.* "You mentioned Jimmy earlier. As I recall, he is your husband?"

I nod. "Yes, that's right."

"You are still married to him?"

I feel this comes as a surprise to her, but she doesn't give anything away in her face or her words. I can still sense it. How would it not surprise her? After all I've done to cause stain in the marriage, you'd expect it would burst at seams and explode. But Jimmy has kept me around, albeit under trying circumstances, and sometimes I am grateful.

"I am."

She nods. I can tell her mind is racing as her eyes are darting all over me. She purses her lips, tilts her head and says, "Have you perhaps considered that Jimmy might have something to do with this? You know, pull a prank on you?"

CHAPTER 17

DR. WALKER'S suggestion sounds unconventional, but I must say Jimmy pulling a prank on me is a strong possibility. I'd suspected him of doing it for revenge, but not for fun—wouldn't he have owned up to it when he saw how upset I was?

Probably not.

She closes our session with a low level of enthusiasm, as if I've wasted her time. I guess I won't be seeing Dr. Walker again. I'm just a burden, a knot that can't be untied.

In the early afternoon, Jimmy comes home with a six-pack in his hand. I'm sitting on the couch, watching him store it in the fridge. He'll be hammered again tonight, his favorite pastime, and my most dreadful one. He is swaying by the fridge door and peering inside. His face doesn't have any expression, so he's content for now. I hate how the house is so small that I can see his every move, his every face expression, his mood. The only time I can't experience Jimmy is when he's behind the bathroom door or in the bedroom. It's a curse we've dealt with for decades, so no wonder he keeps saying he's excited about his new mansion we will apparently be buying soon.

He closes the fridge and walks into the living room, a beer in hand. He gives me a strange look. "Yes?"

"Aren't you working today?"

He scoffs. "Nope."

I stay quiet, contemplating my next response. His sudden quitting of his job concerns me, because he won't get a penny from the lottery money. Once I'm gone, and he realizes that no money is coming his way, I'm sure he will find a job in a jiffy. Good auto mechanics are hard to find, and Jimmy is a darn good one. Meticulous.

Jimmy sits in the recliner and sips a huge gulp of beer. The next thing he'll do is turn the TV on and sit like a hermit all day unless he needs to fetch more beer out of the fridge. I know him too well. I've learned every pattern of his since the day he started beating me. He drinks, he gets drunk; he strikes. Sometimes he is remorseful for what he has done the following day, depending on the injury level, but most times he isn't.

I press Jimmy further. "I mean, does Alberto care you're not showing up anymore?" Alberto is the owner of the car shop he works at.

"Nah. He knows. He said he would do the same thing if he was me."

"I see." I nod slowly. "Well, my shift at Red is today at five. I haven't decided yet if I'm going to quit. Barbara needs me."

"Fuck Barbara." He takes a sip of his beer again and frowns.

I'm afraid to engage too much with Jimmy in case our discussion leads to more questions, so I say nothing. I look at my phone and see it's almost five. The restaurant is a brief car ride from home, but for once, I don't think I need to be there on time. I go to the bedroom and brush my hair. My body is weak and I'd rather stay home and sleep. But fear kicks in when I think of the state Jimmy is going to be in after drinking. Once I'm dressed, I check on Jimmy, who's still in the same position as I left him.

On my way out, I hear him say, "I hope you quit."

I wonder if this is some kind of test. If I quit, maybe all of this will start to feel more real.

When I arrive at Red Urchin, I peer through the windows at the dim interior, and wonder why it's closed. Red is only ever closed on New Year's Day. Barbara would never consider passing on opportunities to make money, even during slow times. But maybe she closed up on a whim today and didn't bother to tell me. After all, her waitstaff have been unreliable lately and would often turn out to be no-shows, only bothering to tell her at the last minute.

I gingerly touch the door, and as I push it open, the lights come on full blast, and the loud scream frightens me. "SURPRISE!"

Barbara is in the middle, and the entire restaurant staff surrounds her, smiling at me. A CONGRATULATIONS banner is spread across the far wall.

"Hey, Lynn." Barbara sounds like she herself has won the lottery. "Congratulations. We're happy for you."

I'm stunned and can barely get any words out for a moment. "What are you guys doing?"

Barbara frowns. "I guess this is a bad idea."

I remain anchored to my spot and don't say a word. A few customers in the restaurant stare at us, some smiling and other looking bewildered.

"Everyone, let's clean this up and go back to work!" Barbara says, avoiding my eyes.

Feeling like I've inflicted pain on Barbara, I turn around to walk out, and out of the corner of the restaurant, I see a familiar figure. The better I focus, the more her features become pronounced. I know who she is. It's the woman I saw at Pinocchio when I met with Greta.

Someone grabs my shoulder, and I jump. It's Selena, the young waitress, also Barbara's niece. "Hey, Lynn. I saw you on the news the other day. Super awesome. Congratulations."

"Thanks, Selena."

"Are you going to keep working here or will you quit?" She lets out a cute laugh.

I shrug. "Maybe. Not sure yet."

Barbara must be pissed after I acted the way I did about her surprise party, and I don't even want to try and picture what her reaction will be when I tell her I'm done with this place for good.

Selena is chatting me up, but I really want to pay all my attention to the woman who was just gazing at me. She has become an enigma I must demystify. When I turn around, she's gone. I head for the door, hoping to catch her and have a word with her. She could have a gun or be hiding a knife in her little purse, for all I know, but I will take the chance. I must find out who she is and why she is following me.

When I exit the restaurant, there are plenty of cars in the parking lot, but I get no clues on which direction she might have taken. I head to the main street, along the beach, and walk frantically, looking for a skinny young woman with long dark hair. The streets are busy, and I keep bumping shoulders with people as I weave in and out of the crowds.

As my steps quicken, I see no traces of the girl. I stop and look in a far distance, hoping to see her, but she's definitely gone.

Disappointed, I turn around and head back to the restaurant to have a chat with Barbara. I hold my breath, trying to get my head around what I'm about to do. I'm about to quit the job that I've held since high school. It's a painful decision, but deep inside, I feel it's the right one. I've appreciated all Barbara's support, even when I was at my weakest.

The familiar smell of sizzling food and the gentle hum of conversation greets me as I step into the restaurant. The place is alive with activity, the clinking of silverware and the soft murmur of diners forming a symphony of familiar routine. I take a deep breath, letting the ambiance wash over me, a stark contrast to the chaos that has been consuming my life for the past several days.

As I approach the counter, my heart pounds in my chest. I have rehearsed my speech a hundred times in my mind, but now the moment is here, nervousness and determination twist in my stomach. Barbara is busy examining a clipboard, her sharp eyes flicking across the seating arrangements.

"Barbara," I say, my voice shaky but clear.

She glances up, arching a surprised eyebrow before shifting into a business-like smile. "Oh, there you are. We've got a busy evening ahead, so make sure you're ready to hit the floor." She's acting like nothing has happened a few minutes ago. She'd never surrender to shame or display disappointment. I'm yet to meet a woman stronger than Barbara.

I swallow the lump in my throat, forcing myself to meet her gaze. "Actually, Barbara, I need to talk to you."

She raises an eyebrow; her smile faltering slightly. "Is this really the best time? We're about to get slammed with the dinner rush."

I take a deep breath, summoning the courage. "I've decided to quit."

Barbara's eyes widen in shock. The bustling energy of the restaurant seems to fade into the background, leaving just the two of us locked in this tense moment.

"Quit?" Barbara finally splutters, her disbelief palpable.

I nod, my voice stronger now. "Yes. I've got a chance to change my life. And I can't keep working here, trapped in the same routine."

Maybe I should tell her about my cancer, but no other words come out of my mouth. Her expression darkens, a flicker of annoyance crossing her features. "And what about your commitments here? We rely on you, especially during busy times like this."

Typical Barbara – displaying an unyielding streak of unreasonableness and selfishness.

"I know," I reply, my voice steady. "But I need to prioritize myself for once. I've been working hard for years, and now I have a chance to make a fresh start."

Barbara's gaze bores into me, a mixture of frustration and resignation. "You're just going to walk out on us? After everything we've been through? Now that you're rich, you no longer need me?" she scoffs.

"Barb, come on, please don't say that. I'm not walking out on you," I say firmly. "I'm making a choice for myself. And I'll help with the transition, train someone else if needed."

The tension in the room is palpable, the weight of our unspoken history hanging heavily between us. Barbara's lips press into a thin line, and I can see the struggle in her eyes—the desire to hold on to me and the understanding that she can't deny me this opportunity.

After a long pause, she finally releases a resigned sigh.

"Fine. If this is what you really want, then go. We'll manage somehow."

I nod, a mixture of relief and sadness washing over me. This place has been my second home for years, and despite all the quibbles and frustrations, it holds a piece of my heart. But the promise of a new beginning, of embracing the unknown, is too enticing to ignore.

As I look around, I remember some of the most intense days we've had at the restaurant. We've been through a lot. Barbara's voice is permanently etched in my brain, yelling out from the kitchen, "Table four ready!"

One particular shift comes to mind. It was the middle of July, and Hampton was in the midst of the busy season. I'm dreading the heat and long hours as I always do this time of year, but I don't mind earning good tips. Tourists seem to be generous tippers.

I run back and forth, drenched in sweat. The restaurant's AC busted a few days ago, and there are fans everywhere, trying to cool the place down. The different food smells agitate me, and I feel like throwing up.

"Table four is ready! Is anyone coming to pick the food up, damn it?"

I can hear Barbara screaming from the top of her lungs, and I wouldn't be surprised if the customers could hear her too. She is high-strung and uptight, but I don't blame her since she's helping her parents run the restaurant.

Thanks to meeting Barbara on the beach a while back, I jumped into workforce when she offered me this job and didn't finish high school. She'd lured me here, promising lots of good tips and good times.

The money is good. I've made so much already that Jimmy and I plan on buying a house together and building a life. Part of me feels like I owe it to Barbara. But today I'm feeling more sluggish than usual. Table four is mine, but I can't bring myself to rush to the kitchen at the speed Barbara expects. I stop near the restrooms and close my eyes for a second. Everything is spinning, and the sounds are muffled and distant. My knees buckle, and I can no longer keep balance. My eyes roll in my sockets, and before I can keep a tighter grip on the wall, I fall and hit the ground. Then I hear a muffled voice say, "Someone call an ambulance!"

Next, I wake up in the hospital, drenched in sweat. The shakes have returned and I'm dying for a fix. I'm disoriented, and I'm not sure where I am. The room I'm lying in looks unfamiliar.

Hours later, the doctor breaks the news I'm pregnant. Two months in already. When I go back to work the following day, I tell Barbara, and she gives me a look of terror. Because I'm young? Unmarried? A junkie? Someone she might lose while on maternity leave? Barbara never had any qualms about making her view heard, and she made it clear she hated me carrying an unexpected life.

Now, all these year later, I turn to leave and I glance back at Barbara one last time. Our eyes meet, and for a moment, I see a glimmer of understanding, a silent acknowledgment of the choices we must make for our own survival.

Walking away from the restaurant, a mix of emotions swirl within me. The decision to quit has been hard, but it is a step towards my resolution to make amends. The lottery win has given me the means to break free from the routine that has held me captive for so long, and as I step out into the world, I feel a sense of liberation I have never known before.

I spend that evening walking by the beach and breathing in fresh air. Sometimes I wish this invigorating, breezy ocean air could just clear out my lungs and make me healthy again. But I know darn well that will never happen.

During the evening, I spend my time going up and down the road like a crazy person looking for something to do. I don't want to go back home and face the drunk Jimmy. His moods have been unreliable lately, and I don't know what I might stumble upon when I arrive.

I spot an empty bench on the periphery of the long road, and I sit down to compose my thoughts. It's only nine, and the air is cooling off. As soon as the sun is down, it's a different climate around here, with the ocean breeze traveling far across the town.

I sit and think about everything that's happened the past few days. For some reason the mystery woman I've seen twice won't leave my mind. Who is she? What does she want from me? My only guess is that she saw me on the news and is now after me and my money.

It's quite a coincidence that I've seen her twice in two days. She must have known my whereabouts ahead of time. Then it occurs to me the only other person who knew my whereabouts was Jimmy. My eyes widen at this realization and sweat beads down my back as fear kicks in. He must have hired this young woman to kill me. A perfect ploy to lose me and get all the money.

CHAPTER 18

MY MIND RUNS WILD. My thoughts are crazy, I tell myself. Wouldn't Jimmy just kill me himself and go live a happy life if he wanted to do that? After all, he'd have plenty of opportunities at home and he's no stranger to violence. But as that thought crosses my mind, I realize Jimmy isn't smart enough to murder someone without leaving a trace. He knows darn well he'd be the prime suspect in the sudden murder of his rich wife and would end up in prison for the rest of his life, kissing the money and his freedom goodbye. He has gotten away with other trouble he's caused, but I somehow doubt he'd get away with murder.

It's a lot safer to hire a hitman. Or a hit woman. Whatever works.

I tremble as I think about all this. I'm frustrated with myself for not being more foresighted. But now my life has become condensed into months, there's not really much time to think about anything, much less about someone conspiring to kill me.

I'm more afraid to go home now than ever. I could sleep in my car, I suppose, but I've done it too many times, and it's uncomfortable.

A thought comes to me: I can find a room in a hotel and stay a night. The season is still low and not so busy, so I might find a vacant room. I'm technically not a millionaire yet, and I have petty cash on myself for a night. But I can use my credit card.

There's a hotel literally across the street from where I'm standing. In the summer, it's chock-full of tourists, day and night. The restaurant on the ground is famous for their lobster rolls in the summer. The hotel also holds functions, like auctions and weddings, and men with fancy suits and women in ravishing dresses parade on the street on such occasions. The season isn't yet in full swing, so I'm praying there are no such occasions tonight and there will be a room to stay.

Before I enter the lobby, I turn around and take one last look to ensure no one is watching or following me. I don't see anyone suspicious. A few people are walking by and minding their own business. At the reception desk, the young man breaks the good news that there's a room available, and "how lucky" I am, considering I didn't call ahead.

He enters my information into the database on his computer, typing at a sloth's pace. I fidget, nervous that someone I know will come through the door. Several minutes pass, and I really want to tell the kid to take a goddamn typing lesson, but I am exercising patience by taking in deep breaths.

He diverts his gaze from the computer and looks at me. "That will be a hundred and seventy dollars, please. How'd you like to pay?"

I rummage through my purse and take my wallet out. My credit card is buried between all the other useless cards I'd once upon a time used and closed out. I still hold on to them, like souvenirs.

"Here."

I hand him my credit card, and he runs it through the slot in the machine. His brows stitch together as if something seems wrong. He looks up. "I'm sorry, but this credit card won't go through. Do you have another one?"

Shit. My face burns with embarrassment. It's in situations like this I realize, sure, money doesn't bring us happiness, but it does bring us comfort and peace of mind. Happiness would probably be easier to attain as a result of those.

I grab another one and hand it to him. He repeats the same and smiles. "It went through." He takes the slip off the machine and puts it on the counter. "Sign here, please, and you'll be all set to go."

I trudge up the stairs to the third floor and find my room. To feel at ease, I lock the door and jiggle the doorknob when I go inside. I'm securely locked and safe here. The room is small and claustrophobic, but that pales in comparison to the rest of the dire situation I've found myself in, and I need to brush off the small stuff. I go to bed, but sleep doesn't come easily. Every once in a while, I check my phone, expecting a text or a call from Jimmy, but there's nothing. He must have passed out on the recliner where I left him.

I feel like a fugitive. I'm a mere few blocks away from my home, but I'm hiding from my husband, who's conspiring against me. If I wasn't convinced before that Jimmy doesn't deserve my money, now I feel it with all my heart. That thought comforts me and lulls me to sleep.

In the morning, I wake up, a little confused about where I am. It all seems like a bad dream. I check my phone. Still no word from Jimmy. I go downstairs and, on my way out, I grab a donut for breakfast. I'm never hungry these days, but I must eat to replenish the little strength I have left in me.

I hope Jimmy isn't waiting for me next to my car, which is parked a few blocks away. As I turn the corner, I hold my breath, but then exhale in relief when I see no one.

I enter the car, and put the engine in gear, looking around again to check for my surroundings before I drive. But I don't go home, even though I very much want to. Home isn't safe anymore, and Jimmy might be in a crabby mood. He may not be drunk, but he'll be bursting with anger that I haven't told him I was going to be away for the night.

I turn left and head toward Best Buy in the next town over. When I arrive, I automatically survey the surrounding space. All is clear. There's little chance of running into someone I know, but stranger things have happened.

The store is nearly empty. I walk around the aisles looking for something that will help me spy on Jimmy. As I turn, my eyes land on some cameras resting on the shelf. I grab one—no, two. No, three is better! I head to the register to pay.

The woman raises an eyebrow when I drop the cameras down. She stares at me, and I put my head down to avoid her eyes. Maybe she knows I'm in grave danger and wonders if I will be okay. And perhaps I'm going too far with this, but I can't dislodge this feeling of danger that gnaws at me.

I take my credit card out and pay for the cameras. I have already accumulated enough debt on the card, but what's three hundred more?

When the store clerk runs my credit card, she informs me it won't go through. I pull one camera out and ask her to try again. Paying for two cameras is not a problem. But my credit card doesn't accommodate the third one, since I've hit the limit. I pay for the third one in cash, the little what is left in my purse. I think I have some more cash somewhere lying around the house, but I'll need to dig. Shit, I've considered staying in the hotel indefinitely until I get all my ducks in a row, but who am I kidding? I'm struggling to purchase cameras, never mind pay for an indefinite stay at the hotel. I have no choice but to live at home with the monster my husband is.

Apprehensive about going home, I drive slowly,

dreading facing Jimmy. It's eight in the morning, so it will be a long day ahead. But when I arrive home, Jimmy isn't there. He usually sleeps on the couch in the living room. I go to the bedroom to see if he might have slept in my bed last night. But he's not there, either. The bathroom door's open, so I would see him immediately if he was here, but he isn't. I look through the kitchen window and survey the small backyard, but all I see is a pile of burned stuff waiting to be disposed at some point.

That Jimmy isn't home gives me relief. I can install the cameras in the places where Jimmy spends most of his time: in the living room. I also place one discretely at the front entrance and near the front door of my bedroom. Thirty minutes after installing the cameras, I feel triumphant that I've accomplished my goal. And there's only one thing left to do.

I go to the kitchen and open the upper drawer. It's been a while since we used the cutlery. Or good knives. Jimmy bought the heavy-duty ones when he was on a BBQ kick and needed to cut big chunks of beef. Like everything else, his interests are always in passing and none of them stick. He has used none of the knives since he put them in the drawer years ago.

I take one out, give it a good look while holding it in the air at eye level. I take it to my bedroom and put it under my bed. Between the cameras and the knife, I should feel safer.

Then another thought occurs to me. To act out on it, I slam the bedroom door shut and lock myself inside.

CHAPTER 19

ALL THE INSTALLED cameras are working beautifully. I connect them all to the app on my phone, so I have visibility of Jimmy's whereabouts in the house at all times. It's almost ten when I notice movement on my phone. Since I arrived home and installed the cameras, I haven't taken my eye off the app in the anticipation of seeing Jimmy.

When he shows at the door, my heart stomps hard. I can feel it against my skull. His face isn't visible, only the back of his head, so I can't tell what mood he's in. I only hope he will leave me alone.

He unlocks the front door and disappears from the view of the front camera and shows up on the one in the living room. He stops in the middle of the room and looks around. His hand automatically reaches for his face, and he rubs his chin as if he's thinking. He shakes his head and looks up, gazing straight at the kitchen. Then he glances up at the ceiling, causing my blood to freeze. His eyes dart all over the place, and I fear the worst. Has he seen the camera? I can see his face clearly. His eyebrows are stitched together, his mouth distorted into a funny contour.

Now I'm certain I'm dead. He'll find me in the bedroom and he'll find a way to kill me. I grab the knife under my bed and wait. My hands are shaking, but inside, I gather the strength I'll need to defend myself should Jimmy strike.

I hold my phone in one hand and the knife in the other. Jimmy disappears from the camera view and enters the new one, the one I'm dreading. The one right in front of my door. He reaches for the doorknob and wiggles it around.

"Lynn?"

I stay on full alert, waiting for Jimmy to knock the door down. He keeps wiggling the doorknob and cussing out. "Lynn, are you there?"

I can sense the concern in his voice, gradually turning into frustration. Then anger. "Lynn, come on, open the door. What the fuck are you doing locking yourself in?"

I pray he will turn around and walk away, but he's persistent. He knows I'm hiding in my bedroom. He can smell my vulnerability.

I walk to the bedroom windows and secure them shut. They are on the ground level, and Jimmy could still break the glass and get through if he wants to. I suppose I can find a simple escape through the windows myself, but they are too heavy for me to lift, especially since my body has weakened. The chair in the corner finds its place under the doorknob for extra protection and resistance. It will slow him down for at least a minute or two until I figure out my next step.

I can hear his heavy breathing on the other side. He turns the doorknob one last time and says, "I made an appointment with a real estate agent at eleven. Get ready and let's go!"

Then a miracle happens: on the camera, I see him turn around and leave. He's not here to kill me after all. He has a different plan for me. It's not perfect, but it's better than killing me.

I hide the knife under the bed and gingerly open the door. Jimmy is in the living room, sitting on the couch, leaning forward and reading something on his phone. When he hears me come in, he lifts his head and sizes me up. "Everything okay?"

"Ye... yeah," I say, "I was just sleeping."

"Sleeping? With the door locked? When did you start locking yourself in?"

"I must have done it by accident." I shrug.

He narrows his eyes at me and shakes his head. "Go get ready. We have an appointment with an agent at eleven."

"An agent? Why would you do that? I don't have money yet."

"You will soon enough," Jimmy proclaims. "Plus, wouldn't it be nice to get a slice of riches for a change? See how rich motherfuckers live?"

"I guess," I say, with a nonchalant air.

Jimmy has dressed to the nines. He is wearing a new pair of slacks and a button-down shirt with flower prints. His hair is perfectly combed to the side, a rare sight. I catch a whiff of his cologne as it spreads throughout the room, and I notice he has freshly shaved. His suntan makes his features more pronounced and his blue eyes stand out. If we didn't have the history like I do, maybe I would fall for him all over again. But our marriage and history are too muddled to be redeemed.

"Go get ready," he says.

"Sure." I go to my bedroom to change. None of my clothes make me look like a millionaire. I finally put on a dress that's good enough, but certainly wouldn't dazzle anyone.

While Jimmy is driving, contentment spreads across his face. His usual tension has been replaced by a small smile as he takes a slow turn toward our final destination.

Big and expensive houses are located only several blocks from us, but they have always been out of our reach. We'd often drive by them, and pay enough attention to know they are grand and inaccessible. That's why, when we arrive at the property Jimmy wants us to see, I'm breathless. The house is stunning, built with white bricks standing out against acres and acres of green lawn. The tall and well-curated hedges surround the property, decorated by various colorful bushes and flowers on the edges. Jimmy is acting cool, as if this is nothing, but I know, deep inside, he is shitting his pants right now.

I look at him. "How much does it cost?"

"Close to two million."

My head spins when I hear the price. This is quite a jump from the run-down cheap rental we have lived in for decades. But I imagine when you're almost four million rich, two becomes just a number.

We stroll through the front yard and reach the entrance, where we can see the breathtaking ocean. The water is calm, and the sun above gives it a glossy feel. In the corner of my eye, I see a woman in front of the house. She's probably our real estate agent. She's dressed in a pencil skirt and a white blouse. Her hair is swept into a bun, and her makeup is flawless. Her eyebrows stitch together, and she makes a face as she squints more closely at us. She must not have not expected two tired-looking, worn-down people to be her clients today.

Jimmy pays her dissonance no attention when he approaches and extends his arm. "You must be Cecilia. I'm James, this is Lynn." He points at me.

At first, she doesn't take his arm, and she looks at both of us, back and forth, back and forth, as if questioning whether she's about to waste her time here. Then, she says, "What can I do for you?"

Jimmy cocks his head to the side. "You can do a lot more if you drop that attitude, lady."

She scoffs. "I'm sorry, but I don't have time to show a property if you can't afford it. Been there, done that."

"Who says we can't afford it?"

She looks at him up and down and jiggles her head. "I guess we will see."

"I just won the lottery," I blurt out.

"Pardon?" Cecilia looks at me, her eyes widened.

"I won five million the other day. Well, it's actually almost four after taxes, or that's what I've been told. I should get the money soon." I play along, even though buying a property is not in the cards. I just want her to see that she shouldn't just make assumptions about people based on their tired eyes or shitty clothes.

Cecilia's face brightens and cracks into a beautiful smile, revealing her straight teeth. "How wonderful. Congratulations. Follow me."

We enter the house; I shake from its beauty. It's perfect. The gourmet kitchen. The primary bedroom with an ocean view. A big backyard with a huge patio and a swimming pool. Another bathroom with a tub, a shower, and a jacuzzi. Three extra bedrooms. A family room with a closed-in porch. Everything is so tastefully built and decorated. I'm absolutely speechless. Until now, I could only dream about being in the presence of such greatness. And now I can afford to buy it.

I can easily picture us living here. As if moving into the house will erase all the terrible memories, the losses, the tears, the years of begetting a life neither one thought was possible. At least the house is large enough for us to hide in our respective corners and give ourselves over to establishing fresh memories, a more beautiful, comfortable life, a more loving future. But it's all too late for me, and Jimmy has no idea.

A small flicker of the happy life we could have

together gleams in his eyes. A blissful stream of new memories to be made that could build us into a couple. He is glowing, and I know he's ready to make an offer. It's been a dream of his to move on from our mediocre life and live large.

"So, what do you think?" Cecilia asks, her mouth all teeth.

Jimmy nods quickly. "I like it. I like it a lot." He gives me a quick look, then back at Cecilia. "I see no reason why we shouldn't place an offer. Right, Lynn?"

Sweat forms on my palms, and my pulse quickens. "Right."

"Well, think about it, and once you decide, call me." She hands us both her business card, even though Jimmy already has her contact information. These little business crumbs might be her strategy for getting closer to the deal.

When we pull out of the driveway, Jimmy says in a singsong voice, "So, what do you think about the house, Lynn? Score, eh?"

I grab the seams of my dress and twirl it around my finger. My heart is beating fast, and I can feel the pulse in my neck. "I don't know."

"What don't you know?" Jimmy jerks his head toward me and gives me a stern look.

"I'm not sure about it. It gives me a funky vibe, you know?" The house is perfect, and I'd give my right arm to live in it, but this is my only chance to discourage Jimmy from pursuing it further.

"What do you mean, a funky vibe? There won't be

houses like this on the market soon. We have to snatch it, or it will be gone before you know it."

"Yes, I get it. But I think we need to keep looking." I need to buy myself time. But my voice is shaky, and my eyes are avoiding Jimmy's, and I know I don't sound convincing enough. "That house is just ... not right."

Jimmy arrives at the stoplight and takes a sharp stop on red. I fly forward and put my hands against the dashboard, my hair getting disheveled by the sudden move. "What the hell?"

"Are you crazy? Are you fucking crazy?" Jimmy's loud voice echoes in the car. "You better tell me what's going on or I'll fuck you up." Anger distorts his jaw. His eyes are glazed and out of focus.

"Nothing. Nothing's going on. I don't like the house, period."

"There's something you're not telling me, Lynn. I know it. Tell me what's going on, or you'll regret it. Don't go down this road again. You hear me?"

I stare at the light as it turns green. The cars behind us honk loudly. Jimmy steps on the gas pedal and takes off at a high speed, gluing me to the back of my seat.

Don't go down this road again. But this time, it's different. Once I'm six feet under the ground, I won't need to face Jimmy and contend with his punishment.

I tell myself that this time it's worth it.

CHAPTER 20

THE MOST BLISSFUL times in our marriage consisted of Jimmy and I planning our future together, excited about what it could bring, how it could change us individually and as a couple. It's hard to believe now that we were once happier, unaffected by the history we have created along the way.

As we speed back to our dingy home, I look back, remembering the exciting moment when Jimmy first dangled keys in front of my face, saying, "Look what I've got."

I'd reached for the keys, but he yanks his hand out of my way, points the keys in another direction and dangles them again. He makes me giggle. "What is it? Is it a new car?"

As a mechanic, Jimmy is in love with cars. He watches Formula One at every chance he gets, and loves going to classic and antique car shows. If I accompany him to these shows, he forgets I'm there. He's worse than a kid in a candy store.

He hugs me and kisses me on the lips. I feel the keys touching my back. I'm giddy with excitement over what Jimmy has in store for us. He pulls away, still holding my arms, and looks me in the eye.

"I've found us a new place, baby-face. A block from the beach."

My eyes widen, and my mouth falls open. I want to pinch myself to make sure I'm not dreaming.

"What? Really?"

He nods and gives me another kiss.

Our current studio is so small that we have no place to store our clothes, never mind build a nursery for the baby, and I'm due in November.

"When do we move in?"

"I negotiated April first. We'll have time to pack stuff up." His eyes dart around the room. "I mean, it's not like we have a lot to pack."

I laugh. "I know. It won't take long at all."

He walks into the bathroom, and while taking a piss, he yells out, "You'll see the place soon. It's great. It's not much bigger than this place, but it's a step up." He flushes the toilet, and without washing his hands, he steps out and zips his pants up.

"That's exciting," I say.

"And best of all, it's much closer to work for both of us."

"Is he going to have his own room?" I point at my belly. We keep calling the baby "he," even though we have no evidence, and we've told ourselves we want it to be a surprise at birth. I've told Jimmy frequently it's a boy because a mother's instinct is always right. Or maybe Jimmy has insinuated several times that he's praying for a boy, and his words have stuck in my subconscious. In fact, he has already bought baby things in blue. A blanket, bottles, pacifiers … he's really counting on me carrying a baby boy.

One day we're having ice cream while sitting on the steps in front of our new rental. My belly by then is visible, and I've gained about ten pounds. Ten pounds, mind you, isn't a lot at this stage of my pregnancy, according to my doctor. At my last visit, she warned me I needed to improve my diet and take care of the baby. Focusing on weight is the least important thing when trying to bring a baby into the world. But she doesn't know that my other, more serious habits haven't changed since I got pregnant. It's a secret I've kept from Jimmy and now from my doctor, as well.

Part of me feels obligated to give birth to a boy, but I don't know how to explain to Jimmy that it's not a decision one can just make.

"Do you really think we're having a boy?"

"We better!" Jimmy quips.

"I've read somewhere that men carry the gender gene." I nod as I proudly spit out this information.

"What does that mean? Like denim jean, but in a different color?"

"No, no, silly. It's, like, when we combine our cells, your cells determine if it's going to be a boy or a girl."

He looks at me with a funny face and scoffs, "That's nonsense."

I shrug. "I mean, that's what I've heard. Don't kill the messenger."

Jimmy flinches at that and gets up. He storms into the house, but leaves the door open behind. I've obviously struck a nerve with him, but as I replay the conversation in my head, I can't work out what I've said that was so wrong.

When I follow him inside, I find him sitting on the living room couch, one leg crossed over the other, while he shuffles through the channels on TV. He's obviously not paying close attention, because he breezes through them, not choosing any to watch.

I sit next to him with some hesitation, unsure of what to say to make things better. He scrunches his face in thoughts, giving away a worry he's been carrying around.

"What's wrong?" I ask. He looks at me and turns away, refocusing on the TV. "Jimmy, please talk to me. What's wrong?"

"It's just ..." he pauses and rolls his eyes up toward the ceiling. "I really want a boy, that's all."

"Okay." I take his hand and squeeze it. I look him in the eye and say, "I promise to give you a boy. Okay, Jimmy? I promise."

He gives me a look that seeks reassurance, so I give him

a slight kiss on the cheek. The second I promise to give him a son, fear grips me like a riptide. While Jimmy's major concern is that I give him a son, my primary worry is that I might not be able to bring the baby, male or female, into the world healthy and alive.

CHAPTER 21

I'VE TRIGGERED Jimmy after casting my doubt about the mansion by the ocean. Our entire car ride passed with him cussing and yelling at me for being stupid for not taking—no, snatching—this opportunity.

We enter the house, me behind Jimmy, clutching onto my purse. My heart hammers hard in my chest, and I'm weak with the anticipation that Jimmy is going to strike me hard. He holds the door for me to go through and gives me an evil eye, his brows stitched together. I lower my head as I hear the door slam, but Jimmy does nothing. He walks by and straight into the bathroom.

I sit on the couch and avail myself of Jimmy. My body is too weak, and I'm all too aware of how my bones are slowly deteriorating. I could never defend myself against Jimmy's force with my health in this state.

He comes out of the bathroom, then storms into the living room, still looking furious. He grabs my arm and leads me to the bedroom. "Get inside." He pushes me as hard as he can, and I land on my hands on the bed. "Don't do anything stupid, okay?"

Jimmy takes the key from the inside of the door, exits the room, and closes the door behind. I hear him working the key on the knob, locking me inside. It's his new way of punishing me. I know it's stupid, but I'm grateful he chooses to lock me in my bedroom as opposed to beating me up. It's an improvement, a step up from the usual.

I open up my phone and the camera app. Jimmy is in the living room, looking around. He sits on the couch and takes his phone out. I think I see the bedroom key on the coffee table. He leans against the couch with his eyes fixated on his phone. It looks like he's texting someone, as his thumbs rapidly move across the screen.

Minutes later, Jimmy is out the front door. His steps look urgent. Then he is gone.

I am so overjoyed that Jimmy hasn't raised his hand at me, it doesn't occur to me until later that I could call 9-1-1 and report the hostage incident or call for help from the outside to get me out of here. God knows I've attempted to will myself and walk into the police station to report all the instances of domestic violence many times before. But Jimmy has such power over me, and he knows it. Whenever he reminds me of what a lying wretch I am, guilt creeps in, and I fold and accept my fate. Not to mention that all his cop friends are on his side and would laugh it off or tell me we should seek therapy.

It doesn't take long for Jimmy to come back. The front door slams shut, and shortly after, my bedroom door is wide open. Jimmy stands at the door, looking at the aftermath of his new ploy. I'm lying in bed, barely moving, and I turn my head to the side to look at Jimmy. An involuntary tear prickles in my eye, and leaves a trail on my cheek.

"Come out," Jimmy says.

I don't want to move, but his commands are not to be reckoned with. What does Jimmy have in store for me now?

He grabs my arm and pulls me toward the living room. I trip on the floor and nearly fall to the ground, but Jimmy pulls me up and leads me toward the couch. He pushes me, and I fall hard on the couch, my head banging against the headrest.

"Where is your phone?"

I rub the side of my head where the pain throbs. With the hand, I pull the phone out of my pocket and wave it in the air.

"Dial this number." He carefully enunciates each digit until I have the full number spelled out on my screen. All I have to do is push the call button, but I don't know who I will reach or why. "It's Cecilia, the real estate agent. When you dial her, tell her you loved the house and you want to put in an offer today."

I swallow a lump in my throat. Jimmy didn't buy my spiel about the house not being perfect. As always, he doesn't care what I feel, nor what I think.

Even if it's a lie.

"Dial now."

Against my desire, my thumb pushes the call button,

and soon, the female voice on the other side answers the line. "This is Cecilia with the Ocean Real Estate Agency. How may I help?"

I dig deep to find the strength to utter the words Jimmy instructed. I'm paralyzed.

"Hello?"

Jimmy kicks my right shin, and I snap out of the trance. "This is Lynn. I saw the big house on Ocean Boulevard today."

"Ah, yes." Cecilia sounds overly happy. "What can I do for you?"

"We ... we fell in love with the house."

Jimmy nods.

"Oh, great!" She doesn't let me finish my sentence, but I'm okay with that, because I'm struggling to say my next words.

"... and we'd like to place an offer."

"Wonderful. Our office is closed on Sundays. How about we meet tomorrow and go over the paperwork together?"

"Su ... sure. What time?"

"I can meet as early as ten."

Jimmy has been listening in. Apparently, Cecilia's voice is loud enough, and he can hear everything. He nods and confirms with his thumbs up that ten is good. The sooner the better.

"We will see you at ten."

"Excellent."

When I cut the line, Jimmy's face cracks into a huge

smile. "Good job, Lynn! We're finally moving out of this shithole for good."

"But I don't have the money yet. How do you think this will work?"

He goes into the kitchen to get himself a beer. While opening the fridge, his voice carries to the living room. "By the time the inspection and the paperwork get done, you'll have the money."

He stands at the door, holding a beer bottle in his hand. "Right?" His eyes darken, and his stare looks sinister. "Right, Lynn? Because that's what you said. You'll get money in two months. Unless you lied again."

I shake my head. "Nope. I didn't lie. It takes that long because it's a lot of money. I've explained this before."

He sits in the recliner and ignores me. I go to my bedroom on full alert. I sleep with one eye open later that night, behind the locked bedroom door, afraid Jimmy would barge in and hurt me.

When tiredness lulls me into sleep, a sound in the middle of the night wakes me up. I jerk out of my dreams and look at my phone. It's only four in the morning. I look around and see nothing and nobody, although I'm sure that something was hanging above me and forced me to be awake. I prop myself up on the elbows and look through the darkness, waiting for my eyes to adjust to it. I see no shadows dancing around. I sharpen my ears to listen to Jimmy, but I don't hear a thing. Is he at home? He usually snores or grunts in his sleep, but it is unusually quiet now.

I step out of bed and head to the living room. He's not

on the couch. I don't remember him sneaking out of the house, although I've been on high alert all night, waiting, putting my hand close enough to the knife to retrieve at the last second if needed.

The shadows of the passersby loom in the living room; a bunch of drunken people walking by our house and heading to their hotel room. It's the familiar scene we're used to seeing this time of year. As my head moves to the left, I notice Jimmy in the recliner, sleeping peacefully, his head resting on his right shoulder. He looks so vulnerable in his sleep.

The rest of the night passes uneventfully. Though nothing in this house is ever uneventful. Every moment is embroidered with a high level of stress and anxiety, and the anticipation of the next fallout always filling the air.

CHAPTER 22

WHEN MONDAY MORNING COMES, I wake up with the feeling of an impending doom. The sun is moving up the horizon, and judging by the amount of light outside, I surmise Jimmy should be at work already. He's always been an early riser, getting to the car shop by six and starting work right away. I rise from bed and rub my eyes forcefully to dispel the drowsiness.

But when I walk into the hallway, I hear a rustle of papers coming out of the kitchen. It's Jimmy. And he isn't at work. He's sitting at the kitchen nook and holding the newspaper in the air. I can't recollect him ever partaking in calming hobbies, such as reading. A cup of coffee sits on the table in front of him. When he hears my steps, he puts the newspaper down. "Well, good morning, early bird. What are you doing up so early?"

My chest tightens, and my head spins. I know Jimmy and I have a ten o'clock appointment with Cecilia today, but I thought he'd take a break from work and meet me at the real estate office. Facing him as soon as I see daylight affects my entire mood. I was hoping he'd already be at work so I can drum up an excuse not to go to the appointment or come up with yet another reason this house isn't viable in order to delay the ludicrous buy.

With apprehension, I walk into the kitchen, shaken.

"What time is it?" I ask. My phone is in the bedroom, an oversight caused by the earliness of the morning.

"It's seven." He takes his coffee mug, brings it up to his lips, and slurps.

"Aren't you supposed to be at work?"

He laughs. "I like your sense of humor." He sips his coffee and puts the mug down, slamming it against the table. "I quit."

My eyes widen, even though I shouldn't be too surprised. I have seen this coming. It was just a matter of time. "You quit? When?"

"Friday. As soon as you quit your job at Urchin."

"How do you know I quit?" I didn't tell him, because, in retrospect, it doesn't make any difference. We didn't make any plans to coordinate our quitting so that we could maintain a stable income until my account hits millions. Jimmy will do whatever Jimmy usually does: think of himself only and accommodate his needs and wants.

"I went to see you on your shift the other night, but guess what, Lynn? You weren't there." He clicks his tongue and narrows his eyes at me. His face brims with hatred. "If you weren't there, then where the fuck were you?"

The comfort I'd had away from him in the hotel room was fleeting. I knew it wouldn't last long.

"I came home late and went to the bedroom."

I look down at the floor and feel like a young girl reprimanded by her stern father. I pray he'll buy my excuse, but when Jimmy slams his fist against the table as hard as he can, I know my prayers are in vein. His face is red as a lobster, and a spittle flies out of his mouth. The mug on the table rattles and creates a loud noise.

"Don't lie to me, Lynn. Do you fucking hear me? Don't ever lie!"

I'm anchored to the same spot, hoping Jimmy will miraculously cool down. If he chases me, I'll run to the bedroom and dive for the knife. I envision him struggling to get up from the tight kitchen nook, which would bide me some time. Jimmy sits still and doesn't move.

"I'm sorry," I say, my voice barely above a whisper.

"Don't say you're sorry. I'm sick of your bullshit."

"Sorry, Jimmy. I won't do it again, I swear."

He stitches his brows together and bores his eyes into me as I sway in my spot, hugging myself, adding a shield. He takes another sip of his coffee and makes a face.

"I quit, so deal with it. You quit, too, and I suppose you don't have a problem with that." He smirks and gives me a deadly look.

Jimmy doesn't know the actual reasons. He does not know I can no longer stand on my feet for hours, or carry heavy trays of food and drinks, while broken in sweat, my wrists bent in excruciating pain. I can't even think straight these days. Even if I hadn't won the lottery, I'd still quit and spend my last days walking along the beach, enjoy the sunsets, savoring the planet as much as I can.

I remain quiet. I nod. "No, that's fine. I'm just surprised, that's all."

"Don't forget our appointment at ten," Jimmy says.

The dreadful appointment.

"I won't." I turn around on my heels and head back to the bedroom. There's nothing I'd rather do than lounge around all day, maybe watch some TV, let the time pass. By nine thirty, Jimmy is knocking on the bedroom door and telling me to get out.

He looks excited. His eyes are sparking like stars. He is so consumed in his own joy, he doesn't notice how unwell I look, not only because I am dying—that's a constant—but also because I have had so little sleep these last few days. We look like the complete opposites of each other. Like life and death. He seems to get younger in appearance; I'm closer to looking like a decomposed skeleton, about to collapse when the attached strings are let loose.

Cecilia won't mind my vile looks, anyway. She's there just to facilitate a real estate transaction, to make us the new proud owners of a house I don't want. To collect a commission.

I will cancel the agreement after we sign it. Maybe on a day closer to my demise.

Jimmy needs to use the bathroom one more time before we leave. I drag myself out of the house, too tired to wear a poker face. As I step outside, a small white envelope draws my attention, and my heart gallops. I grasp it and hold it up, as if it holds some divine message for me. My hands shiver as I open the envelope to see what's inside. When I open it, I see a small piece of paper folded in half. I take it out and read the note:

YOU BETTER BUY THE HOUSE, OR ELSE ...

The note sends a shock of fear through my body. The message is scribbled in ink, in handwriting I don't recognize. So, it can't be Jimmy's. He didn't do this unless he hired someone else to do it. Maybe it's the same person who sent me the flowers and the voodoo doll. The young woman who I saw twice, two days in a row, following me, stalking me. Fear paralyzes me, and I let my instinct lead me.

I lift my head, looking at my surroundings, searching for the culprit. A few people walk by, minding their own business, none of them looking suspicious. I tuck the note in my purse and take out a paper tissue before wiping the sweat from my forehead. The air is clear.

I instinctively reach for my phone to check the camera activities for the past day. Maybe the footage will reveal the person standing on our steps. Even a glimpse of the person might help lead to the ultimate discovery. I'll take the footage to the police station, and they can start the search. That thought gives me hope. I find the app and, with shaking hands, I look for the recorded footage. But I find none. I scoff and cuss under my breath. Apparently, I didn't buy cameras that record. They only give live view access. Are you fucking kidding me?

Shit, shit, shit.

I'm so frustrated with myself and my carelessness. How did I not think of it? My mind has been in a survival mode the past couple of weeks, so nothing I do leads me to a productive and satisfying conclusion.

Jimmy breaks the tension when he comes out of the house and whistles a tune. He's about to secure the house of his dreams, and his happiness is palpable.

Me? Fear is the only feeling I have. I don't want to die before I check off on my to-do list. But here's the irony. I can't complete my list unless Jimmy gives me the information I need. He is the only one who has the key to it. I'm running out of time, so I pray he'll give it to me without asking questions. Maybe I can exchange it for the house if he is amendable to it.

I don't tell Jimmy about the surprise message. Not this time. I suspect all I will get from him is a denial, a sort of confirmation that I'm paranoid or crazy. I'm still convinced he has something to do with this, so I keep it to myself.

I have a perfect plan.

We are silent on our way to Cecilia's office. It hangs on a cliff overlooking the ocean. The water looks as smooth as glass, and the view is breathtaking. But it still doesn't make up for the torment Jimmy is about to put me through. I'm about to commit to purchasing a house I will never step foot inside again. The note flashes in front of my eyes, "or else," so I decide it's better I play along. For now.

Cecilia greets us in her office, wearing a blouse and a pencil skirt, what seems to be her signature look. She invites us to come into her large office, where the view is too distracting for my short attention span. While my gaze reaches far in a distance, Jimmy elbows me and signals with his eyes for me to pay attention.

"So, let's get the offer paperwork together, shall we?" Cecilia's eyelashes flutter as she speaks. She's exuding confidence and femininity, everything I no longer possess. I hate how I'm forced to do this, but if my life is on the line, I have no choice. "Tell me your full names."

My stomach churns and enacts a million somersaults.

"James Corrigan." Jimmy goes first.

Cecilia writes it down, then turns to me. "And you are Lynn Corrigan?"

"No, no." I'm quick to correct her. "I'm Miller."

"Oh." Cecilia's brows rise.

Jimmy gives me a mean look. He still can't forgive me for not taking his last name, what he sees as a symbol of our marriage. It feels like we don't belong; we are not one, as if a name unites marriages. In reality, though, it's just another thing for Jimmy to use against me and to complain about.

"Here." Cecilia extends her graceful arm and places the paperwork on the table in front of us. "You sign here, and you sign there." She points the lines we should sign with her finger. Her nails are long and painted in red, the color I feel my face turn as I'm about to append my signature.

By force.

This is my last chance to say something, to back out of the deal, but I'm feeling helpless. I take the pen, and with a shaky hand, I place my signature on the line. Jimmy does the same, then he cracks into an enormous, sinister smile and looks at me, "Congratulations, sweetheart."

I smile back. "Congratulations to you, too," but I want to puke, and kill him on the spot before disappearing from this terrible situation in a flash.

On our way back home, Jimmy turns the radio on loudly and drums his hands against the steering wheel. He's obviously over the moon, while I'm shrunk into nothingness. My elbow is on the window supporting my chin as I stare into the outside world, the world that seems to have far better opportunities available than life has handed me.

And then out of nowhere, I see her. She's standing on the sidewalk, facing the car, her long dark hair parted in the middle, covering her torso. Our eyes meet for a second, and as the car goes by, she turns toward it, and her eyes follow mine as I turn to face her.

I want to scream and tell Jimmy to stop the car and let me out. But he's in his own world, and I say nothing.

I surrender myself to his actions as he drives me into the figurative abyss.

CHAPTER 23

WHEN WE GET HOME, Jimmy goes to the fridge immediately and takes out a champagne bottle. "Time to celebrate! We're moving out of this shithole soon, baby face. Aren't you happy?"

I'm in the recliner, rocking myself to death, too nervous to ponder what I've just done. I've committed myself to buying a two-million-dollar house I don't want. What pains me the most is that it will remain in Jimmy's possession after I die, the last thing he deserves after all these years. But I can outsmart Jimmy.

I know I can outsmart him.

"What's the matter? The cat ate your tongue?" Jimmy stands at the door, holding a champagne glass, the bubbles inside still settling.

I give him a fake smile. "No, it's just a headache. I'm going for a walk." I get up with difficulty and head for the door. "See you soon."

Jimmy doesn't interrogate me this time, despite having

been extra controlling about my whereabouts lately. He needs to know where I go, how long I will be away, when I will be home. But now I've offered him something that will contain him for a while, he's given up a little of that control. It's like a dangerous dance of cat and mouse.

It's high noon and the sun is bright. Just a few blocks from the house, the beach is at a full capacity, people playing volleyball, women sunbathing, young people surfing, children chasing down seagulls.

I avoid children like a plague. I don't look at them or talk to them. The deep shame inside me knows better than to trigger the memories. It's an avoidance thing, I know. But it works.

I find a spot on the beach away from everyone and pull my phone out. In the browser, I google Private Investigator, and several results come up. I click on my first search and scroll down, looking for a potential PI to work with. The names have pictures next to them. I don't know what exactly I'm looking for. I haven't hired a private investigator before, so I have limited experience. I scrutinize their pictures and assess them by their looks, hoping to choose the best one.

Andrew Lawson, Private Investigator

He looks tough, and he's sporting a trimmed beard and a mustache, and penetrating eyes. That's exactly what I need: toughness. I click on the phone next to his name and the phone rings. I check my surroundings to make sure no one I know is around or watching me.

After two rings, the line picks up. "Andrew."

His voice is curt and deep, exactly what I expect after looking at this photo.

"Hi." I close my eyes, unsure of how to proceed. "Hello."

"Yes?"

"I'm looking for a private investigator."

"That's me." His voice lightens, sending relief through my body.

"I think I'm being stalked, and I need help."

Silence ensues, which makes me uncomfortable. "I see. Are you safe right now?"

"You mean, now, at this moment?"

"Yes."

"I ... I think so." But who knows what will happen when I get home? "I'm sitting on the beach right now. There's no one following me, I don't think."

"If you are not in immediate danger, it's best we meet up and talk. Are you available tomorrow morning?"

If I could find an excuse to get out, I'd be happy with this plan. But living with Jimmy makes my life and my plans all too unreliable and unpredictable.

"I'll do my best. Where? When?"

"Where do you live?"

"A few blocks from the beach, in Hampton."

"Oh, that's nice."

I shake my head. No, it's not, but I say nothing.

"Why don't we meet at Ocean Café near the beach? Do you know it?"

"I think so, yes."

"Excellent. I will see you there at ten tomorrow."

"Thank you."

I put my phone in my pocket and head back home. By now, Jimmy should be half-drunk. My steps are slow, each one adding more fear about my next move. Jimmy can't find out what I am up to. I pull my phone out and delete all the traces of my call with the PI.

Just as I turn the corner, I see Rose tending to the flowers in her garden. I mean to stop in my tracks and turn around, walk to the beach, hoping she'd be gone by the time I come back. But she has already caught my gaze, waving in my direction, holding a small pair of garden scissors.

"Hey, Lynn."

I approach Rose's house and stand on the other side of the fence, waiting for her to shuffle over to me. She's wearing a straw hat, so she lifts her head to uncover her eyes and get a better view of me. I'm amazed at how strong she appears, even though her hump makes her look unwell and slow. But Rose is a rock. A lady who knows how to care for herself.

"Hi, Rose."

"This heat is something else, isn't it?"

There's something in her eyes that sits quietly, like a secret inside she's dying to reveal.

"Yes, it's a scorcher today."

She turns her head slightly to her left. "So? Did you guys end up buying that house?"

A surge of anxiety rushes over me, and I can't help but wonder if Rose is involved in the whole house buying coercion scheme.

"What?" I say.

"Jimmy was saying the other day you guys are buying a house." Her eyes are glassy, boring into me. "Wasn't he?"

"Oh, that. Well, we're putting an offer on a place."

She laughs. "How wonderful." She comes closer and whispers, "And what about Jimmy? Are you going to keep living together?"

Rose must know something. Or she knows more than I have acknowledged in the past. But then, it would take an idiot not to notice the gaps in my marriage.

I nod. "I think so."

She stares at me a few seconds too long, winks at me, and says, "You be careful."

She turns around and walks away, tending to her flowers again.

"Wait. Come back here. What do you mean?"

Rose turns her head and looks at me over her right shoulder. She turns toward me, sympathy crawling across her face.

"Oh, dear. You think I don't know Jimmy has been mean to you?"

She makes a few steps forward and stands near the fence, just a step away from me. She extends her hand and takes mine gently in hers. I silently freak out at her touch. A sob wants to burst out of me, but I do my best to stifle it.

I pull my hand out of hers and yelp, "No." My head trembles. "No, no, no."

"What's the matter, Lynn? Come here, let's talk. I care about you, Lynn."

"I gotta go."

I turn around and run toward my house, hoping Jimmy didn't catch my interaction with Rose. We have known her for so long. I think he trusts her, but with such high stakes, that trust could easily fade.

At home, Jimmy is sitting comfortably in the recliner and watching TV. When I walk through the door, he looks at me over his shoulder. "Hey, Lynn, how was your walk?"

He sounds genuinely curious, as if he suddenly cares about me. I don't remember the last time Jimmy cared about anything I've said or done. But a strange feeling gnaws at me. I'm always wary when people change for the better very rapidly.

CHAPTER 24

IN THE MORNING, I get ready for my meeting with Andrew. I stay put in the locked bedroom until I need to leave, and I give myself enough time to get to the coffee shop. The house is quiet, and I see no movements from Jimmy on my camera app. I exit the bedroom, walking on eggshells and looking for my husband in case he's outside the camera's angle, but he's not here. My shoulders sag with relief. I don't want to explain myself and tell him I'm about to go for another walk. My statement would raise suspicion.

His car isn't in the driveway, which means he went somewhere far away. He's been doing that a lot in the mornings, and I wonder where he goes now he no longer has a job.

But soon I will find out, with Andrew's help.

I come to the coffee shop, clutching my purse and wiping the sweat from my palms on it. I arrive a few minutes late, and Andrew is already there, sitting at a table, sipping from a cup and looking into a distance. He looks the spitting image of his picture, but more rigid and handsome.

Hesitantly, I hover by the table and wait for him to say something.

"Are you Lynn?"

I nod.

"Have a seat."

"Thank you."

He fixes his gaze on me, as if trying to gauge my identity and the real purpose for this investigation. He forms a small smile. "Would you like coffee? Tea? Donut?"

"I'm good, thank you."

The last thing on my mind is nourishment because my stomach is in knots.

"So, you were saying yesterday that you think you're being stalked? Is that right?"

"Yes."

"Tell me, why do you think that?"

"Well. I've received objects and a note from an unknown sender in the last week. It's been happening ever since I won the lottery."

He raises his eyebrows and leans in. "Lottery?"

"Yes. Five million dollars." I place my head down. This is something I should say proudly, but I feel beat and burdened by it all.

"Congratulations." Andrew shuffles in his seat, making himself more comfortable. "So, you believe someone is stalking you because they want your money?"

"Exactly." I play with my fingers as I concentrate on my next words. "I have this awful suspicion that my husband is involved. I've been seeing a young woman in several places, and I don't think it's a coincidence. I wonder if my husband might have hired her as a hit woman."

His eyes dart all over me. "What does the woman look like?"

"She ... she is skinny. Long, dark hair. Blue eyes, I think, although I am not entirely positive. I've only seen her from a distance. She has tattoos on her arms."

"Do you think there's any relation to your husband?"

I turn my head slightly, my eyes down to the floor. I frown, searching my mind for answers Memories surface, but none of the woman I've seen following me.

"No. I don't think so."

"Maybe they are lovers? Has your husband ever cheated on you?"

I shrug. "I don't know. If he did, he hid it very well."

"I wouldn't rule it out just yet, but my investigation will confirm it either way."

I don't know if I should feel disturbed or relieved by this information, but I go along with it anyway.

"Okay. Last time I saw her was when we drove from seeing a house my husband wants us to buy. That was the third time I saw her. I don't believe in coincidences." I shake my head. "I just don't. How she appears everywhere boggles my mind."

"I see your point. But this town is small. I wouldn't be

surprised if she is a local, just roaming around the streets of Hampton. Three times isn't that often at all."

"But the way she looked at me ... those eyes," I choke.

Andrew leans back and watches me struggle with words. "I'll look into this, don't worry," he says.

"Thank you."

"You said you've received a note and other objects recently? Can you tell me more about it?"

I feel stupid, because the day the voodoo doll materialized on our steps, I walked to the closest dumpster in town and flicked it through the air until it hit the bottom, making an echoing sound. The little doll was hideous. It scared me and reminded me of a menacing little creature who'd go after you in your nightmares. I never wanted to see it again, so I had to dispose of it. If Andrew finds out who the secret sender is, the evidence is now gone. Note to myself: I ought not to act on my impulses during these trying times.

And the flowers will be long dead now.

I will focus on the note rather than go into detail about the objects.

"I did. Just the other day. My husband coerced me into buying a house I didn't want, and the same day, I found a note sitting on my front steps, saying I should buy it or else."

His brow goes up. "May I see it? Do you have it on you?"

"Ah, yes." I take my purse and open the pocket where I'd left the note. It's gone. I rummage through the other compartments, but there's no trace of it. I am certain I didn't take it out because my purse was the safest place to keep it. My heart pounding, I take out the contents of my purse and put them on the table—my empty wallet, paper tissues, mascara, my car keys—until my purse is empty.

I look up at Andrew, and he's staring at me with a raised brow, and pity shines from his face. He clearly thinks I'm crazy. I don't feel far from it. Maybe I'm paranoid and I've lost the plot. Though, I'm certain the note does exist. But what the hell happened to it? I must have dropped it somewhere by accident and lost it forever. I wouldn't be surprised given the frazzled state I've been in as of late.

"It's gone," I say, deflated.

"Don't worry," he says. "Here's what I can do for you. I can do some background checks on your husband and carry out some investigation in case it will lead us to the woman you presume is stalking you. If he has any intentions of harming you, he will most likely try to do it soon."

I flinch. My eyes widen in fear, my heart pounding in my chest. "How soon?" I can't have any interference with my plans.

"If I were to guess, the sooner the better for him. But don't worry," he says. "It's preventable, and you will come out of this safe. If we conclude that someone is stalking you, we will involve police and increase surveillance."

"Okay." I nod. "Surveillance is good."

When the words come out of my mouth, I don't feel too convinced.

He hands me a piece of paper and a pen and asks me to

fill out the basic information, such as my husband's name, our home address, and anything else that can aid his investigation. As I fill out the form, I feel like every word I put down is closer to me betraying Jimmy. But it has come down to this: it's me or him. Given how little time I have left, I'd rather it be him.

CHAPTER 25

WITH THE PRIVATE investigator probing into Jimmy's past and present, and the live surveillance cameras all over the house, I should feel safer, but I don't. I spend most of my time in the bedroom fearing the worst and sneak out only when I need to use the bathroom or eat. I watch Jimmy's actions on my phone as he moves around. He rocks in the recliner, drinks his beers, and shifts from the couch to the chair. He seems more unsettled than unusual; almost impatient, and I wonder if it has anything to do with living in this small place now that we've nearly secured a big, luxurious house.

I clutch onto my phone like it's a lifesaver and patiently await a call from Andrew. By now, he should have discovered Jimmy's whereabouts, and whether he has any connections to the mysterious woman stalking me.

A whole day goes by and I don't hear from Andrew. Jimmy, thank goodness, leaves me alone and minds his own business. In the late Saturday afternoon, when couples go out for dinner and enjoy a walk along the beach, Jimmy and I coexist in the pressure cooker, waiting to be spat out. I'm locked in my room, while he is in the living room, wasting his time away. My whole body has become even more fragile and for once, I'm grateful I don't need to work.

My phone rings, and the call display shows an unfamiliar number. The moment I pick it up, I recognize the deep voice on the other line.

"Lynn?" he says. "It's Andrew."

"I know." My voice is a whisper, as I fear Jimmy will hear it and barge into the bedroom.

"Can you talk now?"

"I think so."

"I've investigated your husband, carried out some background checks, and his records are clean. He doesn't have any history of arrest or any criminal activities. Doesn't look like he has even gotten a speeding ticket."

That's because he knows every single cop in this town, and they'd let him go in a heartbeat if he got caught.

Andrew continues, "I also checked his financial records, and there are no unusual activities. Everything checks out fine."

But Andrew doesn't know that he's gotten into fist fights many times. I've witnessed Jimmy instigate scraps with strangers so many times, for the smallest of reasons. Right in the public eye: at the beach, on the street, at the restaurant. He has a terrible temper that can freeze a person's blood, just by sight. That he doesn't even have a speeding ticket shows that he is a criminal in and of itself.

He never takes responsibility for his transgressions, even when he gets away with them. If anything, they enable him to get worse.

Andrew's report doesn't give me relief based on what I know. But there's not much I can do about it.

"No traces of the woman?"

"No. I didn't see anyone with the description you provided. And your husband didn't spend time with anyone."

"What did you see him do?"

"I followed him today and there's really nothing unusual. No unusual places. He's gone to a convenience store and came out with a small bag and a can of soda. Then he went to a pawnshop next town over. He did spend a considerable amount of time in there, though."

"What was he doing there?"

"I came in after he left and inquired about his purchase. The pawnshop owner didn't want to divulge the information about his customers. But..." He pauses. "Excuse me—"

I can hear Andrew cough violently. I wonder what the cause of his cough is. I wonder if it's ever going to be as bad as mine.

"Sorry about that. I'm still getting over a terrible cold."

I stay quiet, anticipating his next delivery of news.

"Anyway, I was mainly interested if your husband might have bought a weapon in the shop. New Hampshire, as you know, is pretty flexible with gun laws. Live free or die, and all that jazz." He scoffs. "But he didn't buy any weapons."

My heart slows down, and I can breathe again. But a strange feeling gnaws at me. I'm having a hard time believing everything he tells me.

"About the woman? Are you sure you didn't see them together?"

Silence carries down the line. Andrew coughs again, more distantly this time as if he's covering the phone. He puts the mouth closer to the phone again. "The woman? No. Like I said, your husband was alone on all occasions. He seemed to be minding his own business."

"That's ... strange."

"I completely understand. But I will continue my investigation, and if in a week I don't find any suspicious activities, I'm afraid I will need to bring it to a conclusion."

I'm certain he will find traces, some kind of evidence that will make all this mess as clear as day. It is just a matter of time.

"Thank you, Andrew," I whisper. "If you find something, please call me immediately."

"Of course. It's safe to say that you're out of reach of any danger. Go enjoy life. Do something fun. Relax." He chuckles.

When I hang up, Jimmy's voice echoes through the house. "Lynn! Hey, Lynn! Come out, I want to show you something!"

CHAPTER 26

I HATE SURPRISES. All my life, most surprises I've encountered have been shocking, vile—ones that have knocked the breath from my lungs, and not in a good way.

Jimmy has a surprise for me. I can feel it in my bones. I unlock the room and gingerly walk to the living room. The sun is on the horizon, and its reflection covers the room in shades of purple and orange. Jimmy stands in the middle of the room, radiating like the sun, his rays attempting to reach me. He is holding a bag in his hand as he extends his arm toward me.

"Here," he says.

"What is it?" I hear the panic leaking from my voice.

"What the hell is wrong with you? Take it." He lifts the bag while his arm is still extended.

I approach him slowly, expecting him to grab my arm and twist it like a pretzel. But Jimmy is smiling; he looks happy and impatient for me to take the bag out of his hand.

I peer inside and see a little box. Jewelry? I give him a

subtle look and take the box out of the bag. When I open it, my eyes widen in a surprise. It's a silver necklace with a beautiful blue opal charm. I take it in my hand and look at it in disbelief. There is no way he meant to buy it for me. He takes it out of my hand and says, "Turn around."

My body shivers, but I oblige. He places it around my neck, then spins me around to look at the foreign object hugging my throat.

"Looks great!"

I automatically glaze over with my fingers and feel the coldness of the metal. I place a tentative smile and, unsure of what's behind this gift, I thank him.

"My wife can't walk around without looking good. I'll tell you that."

His wife won't be walking soon at all.

The palpable feeling of discomfort envelopes the room. I hate it when Jimmy changes his demeanor, akin to a warm day breaking out in the winter. It's a welcome change, but it's so out of place that it's heavy and bothersome.

Jimmy comes closer and cups my face with his hands. "You look pretty with the necklace on. It suits you." He's looking at me, but his eyes are like two hollow circles, boring into me.

He tilts his head and narrows his eyes. "Can we start all over again, baby face?" His voice sounds desolate; his words distorted.

I try to think quickly, but he's knocked me out of balance.

"What do you say?" He caresses my cheek, and I flinch, scared his hand will soon turn into a fist and give me a good punch, like many times before.

What's so different now? Why is Jimmy acting this way? I refuse to be tricked by his sudden act of generosity.

I struggle to say something, but fear erupts inside me, and I remove his hand from my face. I take a step back, but Jimmy doesn't react. He stands stoically, waiting for me to respond. And there is only one way to respond, or Jimmy will morph into a monster again.

I reassure him, "Yes, Jimmy, we can start over."

He comes close and pulls me into a tight hug. "Atta girl."

He taps me on the back twice, like a coach would tap a little child who just lost a soccer game. When couples get in a slump, they revive old memories, remind each other of the beautiful things that got them together, and the reasons they stuck around. Not Jimmy and me. A necklace doesn't serve as the catalyst for resurrecting the good times. Twenty-five years ago, we stopped talking, conversing, sharing like we are just living creatures with no past.

We are shadows of human shells, coexisting.

Jimmy lets go of me and does his usual. He goes to the fridge and pulls out two beers, handing me one, even though he knows well I don't drink. "Come on, take it."

He pleads with me to join him in his favorite activity, as if I'm the type of company he craves. He sits down on the couch and taps the spot by his side, instructing me to sit next to him. I sit down, but all I feel is the tension sizzling between us. He places his arm behind my neck and scoops my shoulder, squeezing it tightly. I shrink like a skeleton. Not only does his touch cause physical pain, but in my mind feels like it could shatter into tiny pieces . His sudden show of generosity confuses me, and I'm unsure how to decline it politely.

Jimmy brings me closer and kisses the top of my head. "Do you believe in fairy tales?"

His voice is soft, like the times he whispered in my ear while lying next to each other in bed, over two decades ago. When we dreamed about the future, our growing family, the beauty that lay ahead. His voice brings me back to that glimpse of happy times, and for a second, I think I have the old Jimmy back.

Perhaps he's finally forgiven me.

His hand moves up to my hair, and he crosses his fingers, sending goosebumps down my spine. He leans closer, just enough for me to feel his warm breath luring me in.

I turn around and his smile mesmerizes me. I try for a moment to trust him, but a voice in my head tells me to remain cautious, to be on alert.

"Do you?"

I shrug my shoulders. "Maybe. I don't know."

He smiles, giving me a look of an angel.

"Let's make a fairy tale, baby face. Let's live the life."

With a dead stare ahead, I nod. It's weighing heavy on me that I haven't been honest with Jimmy about how unhappy we really are.

CHAPTER 27

JIMMY'S sudden new ways of behaving start to bring back more memories. Somehow, the year 1997 is the most vivid one, the one that keeps returning to the forefront of my mind.

Barbara lets me take a Saturday off from my shift at the restaurant. It's April 17th, and the winter hasn't moved on yet. I'm wearing a simple white dress I found at a thrift shop to mark the occasion. Firstly, we don't have a lot of money to splurge on our wedding. And secondly, we are not having any type of elaborate celebration after the ceremony. Plus, the dress I found seems to accommodate the little life inside me. It's not too tight at the belly section. Because we live with modest means, and barely can afford anything major, Barbara has offered an intimate table at the restaurant after our wedding ceremony. She said they would make us a special dinner with lit candles, but Jimmy refused. "We'll go somewhere fancier," he said.

It's cold out, and I put the coat on for warmth. Jimmy is

wearing a suit he's never worn. The icy wind doesn't faze him. We get in his car, and he drives carefully to the town hall. The road is covered in black, thick ice, and the tires are unstable underneath. Complete silence fills the car. I let Jimmy concentrate on driving, but I can tell he's deep in thought. I can see the crevices on his forehead, a sure sign he's been thinking about something important. I don't ask. I am afraid to.

The town hall is deserted from the outside, but when we walk in, another couple is waiting to tie the knot. Unlike Jimmy and me, they are surrounded by many family members and friends, laughing and savoring the moment. Jimmy and I look like the ocean just spit us out and we are looking for refuge from the turbulence. Maybe that's what this marriage is all about. Refuge.

Jimmy says it makes sense for us to get married if we're having a child together. "We don't want a bastard in our family." He said it with a sense of lightness, but to me, it sounds crude and mean. We'd picked a random date for the wedding: April 17, 1997, just a few weeks after we moved into our new home. Things happen in a sequence when a family life is planned: a new place, marriage, pregnancy. We don't do in that same order, but it's close enough.

The ceremony is quick. The officiator asks if we have prepared vows. Jimmy and I turn to each other and shake our heads slowly. No, no vows. We just want to get this done with and go on with our newly married lives. Jimmy pulls me in when the officiator makes our marriage official and gives me a kiss on the lips. "I can't wait to be the father of our baby boy."

Jimmy walks me to the car, holding my arm, so I don't fall on the ice and hurt myself. He is squeezing me too hard, and the pain is throbbing up my arm. He opens the passenger door and shoves me in, like an animal into their cage. We have another quiet ride to what I assume is the fancy restaurant Jimmy mentioned earlier this week. A welcoming and nice surprise.

"Where are you taking me?" Curiosity gets the better of me. We are traveling down the main road by the beach, where many of the restaurants have closed for the winter. I can't think of any fancy restaurants, except for the one in a hotel. But I am beaming because I rarely have a chance to dine at a fancy restaurant. Now we have a good reason to. We have gotten married, and it's time to celebrate.

Jimmy is quiet, presumably focusing on the road, so we avoid an accident. He refuses to answer my question, and I take it that he wants to keep the place a surprise. I smile and focus on the happiness in my belly. Jimmy has already taken the role of a loving and adventurous husband who wants to make his wife—his pregnant wife—happy.

"You know," he finally says. "I just remembered. Darn." He puts his knuckles on his mouth as he contemplates.

"What?"

"Shit," he says, all flustered. "I forgot to make a reservation for the restaurant."

"Oh." I do my best to hide my disappointment, but I

want to be a good sport and assure him I'm fine with that. "Okay, well, maybe next time."

Jimmy turns to me for a second and says, "Sorry, baby-face." But his voice doesn't carry remorse. "Let's just go home and relax. We can do a takeout. What do you say?"

"Okay."

The house is cold. Jimmy turns on the space heater on and puts the kettle on the stove for tea. He insists we use space heaters to save money, even though he knows it's not enough to heat the space and he knows how much I hate the cold. He grabs the cordless landline phone from the wall and dials the number he seems to be familiar with. It's a pizza parlor down the street. He orders a pizza and chicken wings and a salad for his pregnant wife. "It's good for her," he adds, like he's talking to a close friend who gives a shit.

Jimmy puts the music on, takes my hands and pulls me to the floor. The song's name is *You Were Meant for Me*, a new hit by Jewel. He places his hands on the small of my back and swings me gently. His breath tickles my ear as he whispers to me, and I get goosebumps all over my body.

"What should we name him?"

"Who?"

He grabs my shoulders and stares at me. "What do you mean, who?"

"Oh, sorry." My knees weaken, and I feel faint all of a sudden. I hold on to Jimmy tightly to keep my balance. "Sorry. I'm just not feeling well."

"What's wrong?"

I know what's wrong, but I've no intention of telling him what it is. I walk to the couch and sit down to gather my wits. Jimmy turns the music down and goes on with his business while I devise a plan in my head.

By the time we're ready to eat, the pizza and the wings are cold. We sit in the kitchen nook with the food on the table. The lettuce looks wilted. Jimmy is chewing a pizza slice with his mouth open, gazing at me to make sure I don't go hungry.

"Eat," Jimmy says. "Our boy needs to grow strong."

His words sound more like a command than a healthy advice. I take a fork and stab a small tomato in the salad and put it in my mouth. Unease rushes through me, and I'm desperate to flee.

"I'm not feeling well." I get up and head for the door. "I just need some fresh air."

Jimmy doesn't follow me. He stands in the middle of the living room and watches me stumble on the steps as I descend onto the street. It's cold outside, and I realize only now that I've forgotten to grab a coat on my way out. But nothing is stopping me. I march ahead. As weak as I am, I find the strength to move forward, one foot in front of the other.

At the corner of the first intersection with the main road, I turn left. I place my hands under my armpits to keep them warm, but the stiff wind cuts through my face. I can barely catch a breath. Several feet from the intersection, I finally come across what I've been looking for: a telephone box. I grab the phone receiver and realize I don't have coins on me. Shit. I walk into a convenience store a block away and explain I need to make an urgent call. I hold my belly and tell the man behind the counter it's about my baby. He opens up the cash register and hands me two quarters. His face is etched in pity.

I run back to the box and dial the number I know by heart, just like Jimmy knows the pizza parlor's. It's a place of comfort, a place that nourishes him. In my mind, I beg my call to get answered. I'm desperate. I'm profoundly grateful when I hear a voice on the other side of the line. My lips tremble, and my body shivers from the cold, but I find a way to speak: "Skull, can you meet me now?"

CHAPTER 28

A WEEK HAS PASSED when I hear from Andrew again. I've been lucky that the turmoil in the house has calmed down during my patient wait. Jimmy doesn't seem to ask about my every move, though I'm still cautious, taking advantage of the cameras and keeping the knife hidden under my bed.

"Let's meet at the same coffee shop. Can you meet me today at three?" Andrew says.

With nothing better to do all day, I confirm the meeting time. I get out of bed and go to the bathroom to wash my face and brush my teeth. It's almost one in the afternoon, but I've moved around. Jimmy does his usual—he is in and out of the house, planning the rest of our fairy tale. He has been to the furniture store a few times already to pick a new recliner and replace the old one we have, which has been patched up with duct tape in places and stained with the stench of alcohol and old sweat.

I've been patiently waiting for Andrew to call. I

suspect he has a lot more to say and probably wants to meet me face to face for the same reason. The strangely peaceful past week with Jimmy is just a patch of time, a puzzle that doesn't belong. But I am ready. Before I leave the house, I brush my hair to the side and put a bit of make-up on to conceal the depth of my eyes and growing wrinkles and crevasses on my face.

When I arrive at the coffee shop, I find Andrew sitting in a corner, his eyes staring into the distance. I stand at the door for a while and take a deep breath in, readying myself for the dizzying news. He turns around and flinches when he sees me. He waves for me to come, luring me into the new reality I am about to learn firsthand.

I come to the table and Andrew looks at me ruefully. "Sit down, Lynn."

I pull the chair out. The screech caused by the dragging sends anxiety through my body. My face forms a smile, but I know damn well it's a nervous one. I let Andrew talk, as I'm tongue-tied and have nothing to say.

"I've done as you asked me. This past week, I've kept a close eye on James, your husband."

My eyes dart between his sullen face and the coffee mug in front of him, awaiting the punch line.

"Still, there's nothing unusual about his whereabouts. He's completely clean."

Instead of feeling relief, anger erupts, and I shoot, "How's that possible? He has been acting awfully strange lately."

"What do you mean by strange?"

"Well, he's been just too nice to me." As I say these words, I realize I'm opening up a whole new can of worms. I scoff and sink deeper into my chair. Andrew looks at me as if I just grew eight more heads. "Listen, I am just saying that Jimmy isn't the same the last week. He's been acting different, and I'm having a hard time reconciling this change. I feel as if he's preparing something big, some kind of surprise I won't be ready for."

Andrew's eyes get bigger. He picks up his coffee mug and takes a small sip. His eyes are intent on me as he finally says, "I'm sorry you feel that way. But I can't make up stories about your husband to justify your... fear."

"I ... I don't know what you're suggesting here. Please explain."

He glances out of the window, then turns slowly to look at me. "It's not unusual for people to get paranoid when they win sizeable sums of money. I've seen that before. Lots of people who have been through this are living happy and satisfied lives now."

I don't have the luxury of living a happy and satisfied life. "What are you saying?"

"Given there is nothing here to report, I wonder if you'd be better off seeing a therapist, just to put your mind at ease, come to terms with your newly made wealth." He nods quickly, as if to reassure me this is the way to go.

I open my mouth to tell him my mental state of mind is none of his business, and that I've already seen my old therapist, who suggested that Jimmy might have pulled a prank on me. I think better of it and decide not to share.

"But what about the young woman? How do you explain her?"

"If she is stalking you, there's no way to connect her to your husband. But, frankly, it could just be a coincidence that you've seen this woman a few times. It doesn't suggest that she is after you."

"What about the objects and the note I received? How should I feel about those? Someone is obviously after me."

My voice is riddled with fear and anxiety. Andrew keeps a calm face, as if our conversation bores him to death. Then, I remember the last time we met, I couldn't give him the note as proof when he asked me to. He'd looked at me as if I was completely out of my mind. It seems like he doesn't trust what I'm saying. He's staring at me with a look of pity.

"Okay. I guess we're done here, then," I say.

"I wish you the best of luck. I really do. I will send you a bill in the mail."

He's already mid-air, rising from his chair, taking his empty coffee cup to discard on his way out.

"About that. I'm not getting money until a few days from now, so I will mail you a check as soon as I get it."

"No worries." He extends his arm. "It's been a pleasure doing business with you. Take care."

With that, he moves the chair from behind him and storms out of the coffee shop. I am still sitting, motionless, as I watch him disappear from behind the corner. I don't know why, but I feel unsettled. This is the last time I will ever see Andrew. It's almost as if the ground has been removed from beneath my feet, and I'm sinking into the quicksand.

I get up and drag myself out of the coffee shop, feeling the warm air caressing my skin. The tourist season is in full swing and things will get crazier soon. For the same reason, I'd parked my car a few blocks from the coffee shop, which differs from the usual spot in the front.

As I walk, I feel heavy and slow. My eyes fixate on the ground and I count steps, just like I'm counting down the days I have left. I'm also thinking about what Andrew told me, and I'm planning to remove the negative thoughts from my mind. It might be possible that no one is stalking me. It might be possible that Jimmy wants the new start and for us to live a good life. Maybe there isn't any need to be concerned. Maybe Jimmy wants a happy marriage.

I come home and drag myself across the front lawn, which is looking abandoned and unappealing. As I approach the steps, I see a small envelope sitting on the bottom stair, gleaming brightly in the sunshine. My heart quickens, and my palms grow slick with sweat. I bend down to grab and it. Inside is a small piece of paper, folded in half. I open it up and recognize the same scribble from the previous note. With my mouth agape, I read the text repeatedly, grappling with the message.

I rub my eyes in disbelief as I read it once again: **RUN FOR YOUR LIFE**

CHAPTER 29

PANIC SHOOTS through my body like a lightning bolt. The only thing that comes to mind is to take my phone and dial Andrew. My hands are visibly shaking, and the note vibrates in my grasp. I open up my phone and struggle to focus on the task. My mind is stuck in panic mode, unable to move forward. I stare at the phone for a few seconds too long and then finally do what I know I must. I locate Andrew's cell number and push the call button. But as soon as the call resumes, it ends just as fast.

No signal. His line has been disconnected.

My eyebrows stitch in confusion. I dial again in case it's some kind of glitch. But I get the same message again. Andrew's cell number is no longer a legitimate phone number. It remains to be random digits, putting a vast distance between us.

Then I think of the alternative, and suddenly I feel proud of myself. Dire circumstances call for dire solutions. I quickly look up his office number on my browser, and I dial the number listed at the top of the page next to the line: *We got your back. Call now.* The phone rings once, twice, then a woman answers the phone.

"This is a Hampton Private Agency. How can I help you?"

"I need to speak with Andrew." My voice lacks confidence, firmness.

Silence on the other end of the line disrupts my stream of thoughts. Did I get the wrong number?

"I'm sorry, but Andrew is no longer with the agency." The woman's voice morphs into grave, serious, robotic.

This must be a mistake. A joke. I just returned from my meeting with Andrew. He said nothing about moving on from the agency. A million thoughts run over my head in a split second: maybe Andrew was a fluke. Maybe I've missed something obvious. He might have told me he was quitting, but I refused to listen, like I sometimes do. This lady better tell me before I lose it completely. With this new, anonymous note on my steps, my situation has just gotten from worse to fucking terrifying, and I need Andrew to investigate just one more time. Maybe talk police into giving surveillance immediately.

"Do you think you can give me his new cell number? I just dialed—"

"I'm sorry, but I can't help you."

She hangs up the phone.

A stream of emotions overcome me: fear, confusion, but mainly doubt that I will ever make sense of what just transpired. Now that Andrew is unreachable, gone, I have no one to talk to, no one to report the most recent threat to. The note I've just gotten is my ultimate sign, and I must do something. It's the ultimate confirmation of what I've feared all along. Jimmy is just putting on an act as an improved husband to conceal his little ploy to get me killed. It's picture-perfect, akin to stories from murder mystery books. Everything makes sense. I need to get away from him as fast and as soon as possible.

But I can't do anything until I get the information I need from Jimmy. I'd better do it today.

That same afternoon, a message on my phone pops up. The one I have been waiting days for. The one that will make my life easier. It's from my bank. I log onto my account and see the money has arrived. All of it. All three-and-a-half million dollars and change.

I'm sitting on my bed and feeling so excited that I want to scream, but I can't blow my cover. Under no circumstances can Jimmy find out about this. Now I can execute my plan.

Time has finally come.

I contain my excitement before I head through the door. Jimmy is sleeping in the recliner in the living room with his mouth agape, saliva drooling down his chin. I don't want to wake him, so I sit on the couch and wait. He is breathing silently, and his chest is moving in a steady rhythm. As I watch him, I wonder if he is dreaming, and if so, if his dreams are pleasant or disturbing; if they resemble any of his reality or if they paint a brand-new world. It's been a long time since I've viewed Jimmy as a human.

Sleep makes people look innocent, content, beautiful. The rest of his body is dead-looking, silent, as if the parts don't belong to him.

Out of boredom, I turn the TV on and mute it. Local news is on. It's almost six in the afternoon, and I'm getting eager to probe Jimmy. He shifts in the chair and slowly peels his eyes open. The reflection of light from the TV makes him grunt. He turns to me. "Hey, what time is it?"

"Almost six." I reply with my fingers. I'm terrified about the conversation we're about to have, but it must happen. It's been decades, and I deserve to know.

Jimmy is rubbing his eyes with his fists. He's smacking his mouth, as if he has something sweet on his tongue, but he's probably just cleansing himself from the dreams.

I can never be ready for the next steps, but I forge ahead.

"Jimmy, I need to ask you something about our son. Will you tell me?"

He gives me a stare, etched with confusion. "Tell you what?"

"I need to know, Jimmy. I need to know. Tell me. Tell me. Please."

Jimmy falls silent. For the first time in a while, his silence irks me. I can tell he's thinking, ruminating over the question. My pleads only seem to make him angry. "What the fuck are you talking about? What do you need to know?"

"I need to know where you buried our son. Where? Where, Jimmy?" My voice sounds desperate, whiny.

He jumps out of the recliner and rushes over to me. Suddenly, he no longer looks sleepy. Or human. He grabs me by my arms and pushes me as hard as he can toward the floor. My body slams into the floorboard, contorting into a strange shape. My hair looks disheveled and crazy. Tears stream down my face. I prop myself up and kneel, facing him.

"Please tell me where you've buried him." I cry hysterically, and my voice echoes in my head.

"I told you a million times not to mention it!" He comes near me, grabs my shoulders, and starts shaking me. "How many times did I tell you not to talk about it? How many?"

I get myself out of his grip and place my head on the floor. Jimmy takes a few steps back, leaving me alone to my pain. My whole body convulses as I hyperventilate.

"Don't you ever mention it again, or I will kill you."

I can't see Jimmy, but I can tell he is talking through the clenched teeth. It's the threat I've heard so many times before, but it has never rung as true as now.

"But why? Why?"

"Because. Because … it's all your fault!" Jimmy turns around and exits through the front door. I pick myself from the floor and drag myself to the bedroom. He comes back soon after, opening another beer.

Inside the bedroom closet is a duffel bag I've stuff with a couple of T-shirts, a few sweatshirts, and a couple of pairs of pants. I stay put, locked inside the stuffed room that evening, spying on Jimmy with the live cameras. He finally falls asleep around one in the morning. I wait for Jimmy to fall into a deep enough sleep not to flinch at a notable sound.

Around two in the morning, I walk by him, and exit through the front door, the duffel bag strap over my shoulder. I rush through the front lawn lit by the moon, enter the car, rev the engine, and—to my relief—I flee.

CHAPTER 30

I ARRIVE at a hotel two towns over where Jimmy can't find me. The hotel is rated five-stars, overlooking the incredible ocean sites and coastline. On the outside, like the stars suggest, it looks fancy, nothing like some shoddy boutique motels along the beach in Hampton. Jimmy would never suspect I'm here, not in a million years. I've passed this hotel many times before, always imagining who might stay here. Maybe rich people visiting out of town, or businessmen coming for a conference. Now that I can afford to stay here as long as I want, I find solace in the thought. I park in the lot behind the hotel, under a tree and away from the entrance, where Jimmy would be less likely to find me.

My room looks clean and inviting, nothing like my home. I've picked a suite with a king-size bed, ocean views, and a jacuzzi in the bathroom. I could use a relaxing bath later on. First, I hit my head on the pillow and cocoon myself between the sheets. They smell fresh and airy—

lavender, I think—and they lull me to sleep. For the first time in a while, my bones feel fully rested. My body shifts into full relaxation, as if all the tension has been released at once.

I sleep in, and it's almost ten when I wake up. I look at my phone and see messages from Jimmy. He's called me several times and sent me umpteen texts, asking about my whereabouts.

With sleepiness in my eyes, I open up the cameras on my phone to watch Jimmy. He's sitting on the couch in the living room, holding his phone and texting. Seconds later, I receive another text from him. I can see his face, morphed into rage, as if he's about to erupt. No sounds come through, but I can read his lips as he says, "Fuck, fuck, fuck." He stands up from the couch and punches the wall. I imagine he wishes that wall was me right now.

A sudden unease washes over me.

In my frenzy this morning, I forgot to take my most valuable possession, my charm which I've kept all these years. It's the only thing that connects me to my dead child. Because, I don't even have memories. Not one. I'll have to go back home, but I will need to wait for Jimmy to leave the house first. I train my eyes on the camera and wait. Jimmy is walking around the house like a chicken with its head cut off. I can only imagine what it feels like to no longer be able to take control of the situation, or of me. As he moves from one room to another, he goes in and out of the camera view. Finally, he crosses over into the living room and heads for the exit door. In the entrance camera,

Jimmy skips the front step like he is in a rush to be somewhere. As soon as he disappears from my view, I launch myself from the bed and head out of the hotel. I drive home, nervous about how my quest to accomplish my goal will play out.

Upon returning to our street, I position myself at the intersection, scanning to see if Jimmy's vehicle is parked in the driveway. It's not. I sigh with relief, and I make a quick plan to be in and out of the house. As I approach the front door, I feel as if I am a murderer returning to the scene of murder I committed. With each step I take, the tension rises in my body, as I fear Jimmy will suddenly turn up and punish me for leaving him last night. In his mind, he's probably thinking the house we put an offer on is no longer his. The promise of a better life is eliminated like it never even existed.

The front door is unlocked. Jimmy forgets to lock the door often, not that anyone would bother to break into our house. If they did, they'd be disappointed just to see useless items spread out on the floor, and tasteless furniture that needed replacing a while ago. As soon as I enter, the smell of doom splashes over me. We haven't aired the house in a while; the windows have been kept locked for months; the deep clean hasn't happened in years. After spending the night at the hotel, it's taken only a day to realize this; to see a difference between good and bad. Rich and poor.

I go into my bedroom and notice immediately the bed has been stripped naked. The covers are lying on the floor, crumpled into one gigantic pile. Jimmy must have come in this morning to look for me and done his usual rampage. As much as I want to neaten the room, I realize it's pointless, so I leave the pile as it is. I approach the closet and open the door. There in the corner, I see the bag I've come here for. It's the one that contains memories, prospects, the fleeting potential of another life. Without looking back, I quickly grab the bag and run out of the house.

My wish is to never have to come back here, to never again feel the suffocating fear this house radiates.

Before I run to my car, which I parked on the street for a quick exit, I hear my name. My heart pounds hard. It's the voice I have heard so many times before.

Rose.

It's the worst timing. She's standing at the fence in front of her house and repeats my name. "Lynn. How are you, dear?"

Our last conversation comes to mind, and I wonder if she wants to readdress it. I sure as shit hope she doesn't. I have no time

"Hi, Rose." I hold the bag against my chest as if I just stole it. She gazes at it, and I can tell she's wondering what I'm holding.

"Are you in a rush, dear?"

"No." I shake my head. "Well, yes, I am kinda. What's up?"

"Are you getting ready to move? Is that something you're moving to your new place?" Her eyes gaze at the bag.

"Yes, this is coming to the new place."

"How wonderful. I'm excited for you. I can't wait to see the house." Her voice reduces to a whisper. "I hope you will let me visit you, will you?"

"Of course." My eyes divert from our surroundings, looking out for Jimmy in case he appears and decides to storm in my direction.

But Rose gets my full attention when she says, "I saw Jimmy this morning talking to the real estate agent."

"Real estate agent? Where?"

"Right here, in your yard."

My blood freezes. We never have any visitors, so the probability of it being Cecilia who came over is high. What was she doing in our yard, and what did she have to discuss with Jimmy? Fear runs over my body, and I look at Rose in dismay, "Oh, yes. They were just discussing last-minute plans."

She leans in toward me. "Your real estate agent … she's so young."

If Rose considers mid-forties to be young, then I completely agree. But a strange feeling gnaws at me, and somehow, I think Rose is not referring to Cecilia at all. I tilt my head and say, "How do you know she was our real estate agent?"

She smiles. "I spoke with Jimmy later. He said so."

It doesn't answer my question as to why Cecilia would stop by, but I play along. "Was she wearing a pencil skirt and a blouse?" I add a small laugh to relieve the tension.

Rose bows her head and shakes it slowly; her eyes

focus on mine as she delivers the words that shake me to my core. "No. She was wearing a tank top and a pair of baggy pants. For a second, she didn't strike me as a real estate agent. You know, her tattoos and her long dark hair? There's no way in hell she's a real estate agent."

CHAPTER 31

I'M DROWNING IN FEAR. It takes over me like a sudden tornado, swirling around, unapologetically taking everything in its path. The woman Rose just described resembles the looks of the young woman who has been stalking me. I have no doubt that Jimmy and she are in cahoots with each other, plotting to find and kill me.

I say goodbye to Rose, slide into my car seat, and head toward the hotel. As I'm driving, my eyes dart between the road and the rear-view mirror. In the mirror's corner, I see my eyes, and the agony etched in them. I can't shake off the feeling that someone is following me, intending to strangle me.

There is no doubt in my mind now that the woman exists. I've seen her. Rose has seen her. She exists. And she is out there to get me, plotting with Jimmy against me. There is no doubt they are after my money. My fear has multiplied, and everything feels more immediate, more urgent.

I am driving, but I'm also having an out-of-body experience. My moves are automatic. I'm dying to reach shelter, my makeshift home, a small suite in a corner of a fancy hotel. I arrive there, sighing with relief, power walking through the lobby. My room is on the fifth floor, but I don't care to take the elevator. I have no time to spare. I take the stairs up, but my steps are heavy. My weakened hands grip onto the railing as I push myself forward, my feet dragging behind. Every so often, I cough, which, as of late, has gotten worse and more frequent. As my health deteriorates, I'm becoming more intent on making my last wish come to fruition.

I want to visit my son's grave. For the first and last time. I want to touch it, say a few words, tell him I am going to meet him soon.

It's not like I haven't looked for his grave before. I have. On several occasions. Last time I did it, I arrived early morning, where the cemetery was drenched in the sunshine, giving it a heavenly feel. The cemetery is huge. At least thirty acres, a home of thousands upon thousands of dead bodies, some resting there since the eighteenth century. Some of those gravestones are so old, the engraved letters are faint, erasing the names of the people as if they never existed.

The rows of graves stretch endlessly in every direction, and the tombstones seem to mock me with their indecipherable inscriptions. Panic starts to rise within me as I frantically read each name, but my son's grave eludes me, slipping further into the labyrinth of the cemetery's depths.

And then, just as I'm about to give up, the heavens open up, and a torrential downpour begins, drenching me to the bone. I'm forced to abandon my search, my tears mixing with the rain as I retreat, the chilling realization settling in that my quest for closure may forever remain incomplete.

In the room, I place the bag on the bed and open it. It hasn't been touched for decades, and I'm finally ready to face it. My heart pounds in my chest, and I close my eyes and take a deep breath to compose myself. I pull out the tiny blanket, now looking sad at its old age. It no longer smells of a newborn, but of the old, stale, moldy stench it's collected in the corner of a closet. I take it in my hands and hold it to my face. It's wet, and I am confused why. Then I quickly realize it's my tears streaming down my face.

I can only imagine what life would be like if he were still alive. I try to picture his facial features, his personality, whether he would resemble Jimmy or me. All these years, I've held him in invisible arms, hugging him, squeezing him, loving him. Ever since the dreadful loss, I've kept him close to my heart, longing to touch him.

I wonder what kind of family life we would have. Jimmy, our son, and I. I picture us walking on the beach, looking for shells, playing with the beach ball, fighting the ocean waves while laughing in unison. Then we'd go out for dinner, all three of us exhausted from a good day, and happy in our own little familial world.

I haven't allowed myself to dream what it could be until today.

I ruined it all.

The sound of the heart machine in the hospital still rings in my ears. The IV needle hooked into the vein of my arm was a reminder of why the baby didn't make it. Every time the nurse came into my room, I flinched. Each time the door opened I hoped it would be different that time. Maybe the nurse would hold my baby, hand him to me with a smile on her face. But no such luck. She'd come in empty-handed, hurriedly checking up on me. She knew I'd failed as a mother. As a human being. Women like me don't deserve respect when selfishness leads to the murder of my child.

Jimmy is right—it was all my fault. The guilt I've lived with is stronger than any imaginable feeling I've ever experienced.

Tomorrow, I will seek his grave. There are only a handful graveyards in the Hampton area, and I'm determined to look, even if it takes days. When I find it, I'd love to build him a gravestone with a message engraved on it. I'm still thinking about what it could be, but something simple and meaningful comes to mind. Something like: *"Into eternity's embrace, you soar on the wings of our memory, a beloved son whose light forever guides our hearts."*

I consider a million variations of the same message but can't settle on one. Maybe it will come to my dreams. Maybe my angel will whisper it to me.

The heavy thoughts wear me out, and I force myself to get in bed and rest. I close my eyes and let dreams carry me.

CHAPTER 32

I WAKE up in the morning, greeted by silence. There are no threatening texts from Jimmy. It's unusual, but I find relief in it. I get up and go get breakfast and coffee to perk up. The buffet spread sits in a corner of a large room on the first floor. I grab a hard-boiled egg and a muffin, a cup of Starbucks coffee and head back to the room. Through the window of my room, I see the ocean glistening, the sun moving up high, beckoning.

After I eat my breakfast, the first thing I do is open up the cameras to spy on Jimmy and see what he's doing. I see Jimmy sitting in the recliner, a big smile across his face. He's gently rocking and staring ahead, but I don't think he is watching the TV. He's looking in a different direction. His smile and vacant eyes are as creepy as hell.

What is Jimmy up to now? He looks pensive, as if he's plotting something sinister—or has plotted already—and is just waiting to enjoy the fruits of his labor. Something is different about him. Then, suddenly, he looks up and stares right into my eyes through the camera.

I scream.

The phone drops out of my hands and the uncontrollable scream continues coming out of my mouth. It's the primal scream coming from deep inside of my gut. I cup my mouth with my hand, afraid to draw the attention of the hotel staff and visitors with my terrifying howls. Jimmy blew my cover, and he knows I've been spying on him.

He has found the cameras.

I'm certain I'm the next one he will find and destroy. I'm dead. It's just a matter of time. I know my soon dying is inevitable, but I want to die in peace, and not at Jimmy's hands. If I can help it.

It's clear he has waited for me to discover this, and for our eyes to meet. I'm shaking even though I know he can't see me. I grab the phone and keep watching Jimmy staring at the camera. Then he stands up and trudges toward it. He gets so close that all I can see now is his face, looking distorted. I can't see his full features, only his enlarged nose and his moving lips. He is obviously speaking, but my dizzy mind cannot read his lips.

I check the views of the other two cameras and nothing comes up. An error message. He must have found and disconnected them already. No, not just disconnected. He must have torn them out with all his raging force and threw them onto the floor, shattering them into hundreds of small pieces.

Seconds later, Jimmy's hand comes into close focus,

and the camera goes off. The screen turns black. I can picture him throwing the camera against the wall, cussing me out, calling me the worst names, like he always does in a wave of rage. If I were at his arm's reach, he'd be putting his revolting claws on me, tearing me down.

The panic I'm feeling is too much to bear. I run into the bathroom, see my fearful face in the mirror, then sprint back to the room, unclear about my next steps. I jump on the bed, get under the covers, bury my face in the pillow and scream. Somehow, it releases the internal tension, but I'm still visibly shaking. I have avoided death under Jimmy's spell so many times, but it has never felt as real as it does now.

Within the confines of the room, I tell myself I am safe. Jimmy can't get me. He cannot find me or trace my steps. I can go on with my business today, as intended. I can go look for my son's grave. Pine Grove Cemetery. In a distant memory, I've heard Jimmy utter these words before. Both my parents were buried in the Pine Grove Cemetery, which is on the periphery of Hampton. I will most likely be buried there as well. Which reminds me, I have to plan for my funeral.

When I step outside, the day looks inviting and beautiful. The strong wind picks up, and the ocean makes belligerent waves, sending a reprieve to the heat we had the past few days. I sit in my car and pull my phone out, putting the Pine Grove Cemetery address in the GPS. It's been a while since I visited my parents' graves, the weight of their absence feeling almost unbearable each time, like a persistent ache that refuses to heal. It's a fault of my own, just like failing to find my son's grave in all these years. I don't think I remember to get there without directions. According to the GPS, it's a twenty-minute easy ride from the hotel. The traffic looks clear, with only a couple of orange and red short lines along the road.

I focus eyes on the road and suddenly, a knot in my stomach forms. I'm not entirely ready to face the grave, but I must. Ever since I've lost him, I've been thinking about getting him a special gravestone with the image of an angel and an epitaph. Maybe plant a couple of flowers to liven his grave. All these years, I couldn't afford any of it. Everything I earn in the summer months gets stretched over a year, and all I can afford is the necessities, like food and splitting monthly rent with Jimmy. But now I'm rich I can afford it, and I don't think it's ever too late to do something in his memory.

The GPS takes me on a highway, what seems to be a detour to my final destination. There has to have been an accident on the main road. I take the exit and enter the vast, empty road ahead of me. Ten minutes, and I will be there. The directions tell me I should take the second exit. As I approach it, my heart beats faster. I turn the radio on, but as soon as I do, I shut it down. I'm too nervous to concentrate, or to listen to it. It won't distract my wandering mind, and it definitely won't put me at ease.

I take the exit onto a windy road, and I nuzzle the brakes to slow down. But under my foot, I feel something is wrong. The brakes feel loose. They are not doing what they are supposed to do. Slowing down. I push them again, with a little more pressure this time, but nothing changes.

The car is still going at a full speed. I try to steer in the right direction, toward the ending tail of the exit, but the car is going too fast, and I can't keep it straight. I weave on the road like a drunken person on a street, and seconds later, I completely lose control of the wheel.

First, fear kicks in. It feels like riding on a malfunctioning plane, spiraling into the abyss. With every passing second, death gets closer. Then, survival mode kicks in, leaving fear behind, and I hold on to the wheel to steer it in the direction that might help save my life. Afterward, I make my way over the small field that separates the lanes going in opposite directions. I fly through it until a car coming in the opposite direction stops me with a full-on collision. The airbag dislodges itself out of the steering wheel and hits me in the face. My neck jolts painfully as my head is knocked backwards.

My head feels heavy, and my mind is clouded. I feel like I'm about to lose consciousness, but I fight it.

Even with a clouded mind, a clear thought occurs to me and causes my body to tremble. Jimmy took my car for a check-up and repairs only a few months ago. The likelihood of the brakes malfunctioning should be slim to none. Then it occurs to me. This is all a setup.

A plot to kill me.

A ploy to destroy me.

It becomes as clear as day.

Jimmy has found me.

CHAPTER 33

THE POLICE and ambulance sirens rattle my eardrums as they approach. My head is still resting on the seat, and as I blink to keep myself conscious, Jimmy's smirk from this morning flashes in front of my eyes. He must have found my car in the parking lot at the hotel and messed with the brakes. It's the easiest way to send someone to death and get away with murder.

But I'm alive. Still breathing. I think.

The EMT opens the door with difficulty, as according to the shouts I can hear from outside, the collision caused the car to look like a chewed piece of food. It's been totaled, and so has the car I collided with.

"Are you okay?" the EMT asks.

I nod, but I'm not sure. I look down to see if my legs are still attached, but all seems fine. Bruises and some other injuries will undoubtedly surface soon. I'm dizzy, yet happy I survived the crash.

He unbuckles me, shifts me to my right, and takes me

under my armpits to pull me out. He does it with ease, then he carries me like a child, and puts me down on the stretcher. I look up at the sky, murky from the impending rain clouds. I almost want to laugh at the number of things that have gone wrong in my life, one after the other, even when I'm trying to make things better for the short time I have left. Everything has piled up into a big, shitty heap.

"Lynn?"

I move my eyes to the left and see a cop standing nearby. "Is that you?"

I see a man in a cop uniform, but I don't recognize him. When he gets closer, I see Danny, a local cop who comes to Red Urchin often. He's one of those guys whose company you crave, always a smile on his face, a good mood that's contagious. Barbara has served him a meal for free many times, but sometimes I wondered if there was more to it. Could it have been some kind of bribe for favors Danny has done for Barbara? Who the hell knows?

The last thing I want is for Danny to see me lying on the stretcher, banged out, barely alive. I give him a small wave with my fingers, and that's the best I can do at the moment.

"They are taking you to the hospital. You'll be okay." Danny's face hovers above me. He looks concerned, as if there's something on his mind he wants to tell me.

I nod and smile. He waves back and leaves his hand up in the air as he watches me moving out of his sight. The EMTs slide me into the ambulance, and seconds later, we head to the hospital with the sirens blasting through the town.

They take me to Portsmouth Regional, where I gave birth to my son, where my dreams got crushed. As they wheel me inside the hospital, a sense of trepidation overwhelms me. The nurse takes over and wheels me to an urgent care room where they take patients. The commotion in the hospital is dizzying, almost unbearable. Nurses in their scrubs rush from patient to patient, trying to save their lives. This place gives a horrible vibe. A combination of the sudden memories flooding into my mind, and the terrible condition I'm in. It's like I'm hanging onto a life thread, and it's about to sever any second.

The young doctor checks up on me. Hours later, after endless examinations and scans, I'm told I've got whiplash and a spinal cord injury. The cancer had already worn my spine out, leaving it vulnerable, so this result was pretty much inevitable after an accident of this magnitude. The throbbing pain dials up further by the minute, and my mouth is super dry. I'm dying for a glass of water, but a grunt is the only thing that comes out of my mouth. The nurse seems to have read my mind and brings me a small plastic cup of water. She lifts me up and helps me drink from it. The water gives me a surge of energy, and I'm finally able to focus on something other than the pain and my parched throat. I can even see everything better, including the concern on the young doctor's face.

"You need to stay at the hospital to be watched until

your injuries heal," the doctor says. He turns to the nurse standing nearby. "Lindsey, move her to a room upstairs."

"Wait, no." I find my voice.

He jerks his head toward me and tilts it. "Excuse me?"

"You need to release me from the hospital. I've got something important to do."

He comes closer and takes my hand. "I'm sorry, but I'm afraid you don't have the option. You must stay."

Being forced to stay at the hospital couldn't have come at the worst possible time. There's no way I can stay here, glued to my assigned, uncomfortable bed, while I have a million things to do. I'm at my breaking point and the doctor doesn't seem to understand that I have no time to waste. I can't convince them, so they wheel me to my new room and instruct me to rest.

I fall asleep almost immediately, my body fully relaxing, regardless of the turmoil inside me. It's doing what it needs to in order to recharge its almost empty batteries.

When I wake up, it's past midnight. I'm lying in my hospital bed, feeling the tension in my bones. The IV is hooked into my arm, a reminder of the days the needles were my best friend. For the first time, I stupidly feel grateful for that experience. It will make my escape from the hospital much easier. I remove the tape from the IV and slowly ease the needle out of my arm. Climbing out of bed inch by inch is agony, and I have to bite my lip to stop myself screaming in pain, but I manage to shuffle to the door without incident. Then I remember my clothes, and curse as I creep back to retrieve them from the cabinet in the corner. I won't get changed here, I'll find a bathroom I can lock so I won't be discovered or held up by the nurses.

Outside, my room is quiet. There's only one nurse on the floor—a shortage of staff, they said earlier— so I don't expect anyone to be checking up on me. They already know I'm dying of cancer. Is there a reason to care? To save my life? We all know the answer to that.

The hallway is dim and growling sounds emanate from the rooms on either side. It's terrifying to listen to people's suffering. They should be sleeping peacefully now, but life has a different plan for some of us. I arrive at the ward door and find my first major obstacle: the heavy double door is locked, and there is no way out. Shit. I've always hated hospitals. They treat you like prisoners. Just as I'm about to turn around and search for an alternative exit, I hear footsteps coming my way. I hide behind the wall in the corner and wait for the steps to get closer.

I'm so weak I feel I'm about to collapse, but the adrenaline keeps me going.

I hear a push of a button and the doors opening. I peek from the corner and see a nurse exiting through the door, rushing to her destination. Just before the door closes, I creep around the corner and manage to shuffle through the gap. The nurse has already disappeared around the corner of the wall. The coast is clear. I go to the first bathroom and put on my clothes. Peering into the mirror, I fix my hair. God, I look horrible in this weak body, but I tell myself all will be over soon. I discard the bag my clothes had been in just a few minutes ago and head outside.

When I step onto the street, the rain is falling down with vengeance. I call an Uber, which arrives a short few minutes later. It's almost two in the morning, and the streets are empty. I slide into the car and watch the town veiled in black while clenching my teeth as every rattle of the car sends shockwaves of pain though my every nerve. When we arrive at the final destination, I thank my driver and exit, slowly prepping myself for the onslaught of water pouring onto me.

Then I step in front of the house and I exhale deeply.

CHAPTER 34

IT'S good that it's pouring with rain tonight. It makes people stay inside. It disguises things.

It's almost three in the morning, the devil's hour. The neighborhood is sound asleep. I'm standing in my front yard, soaked to the bone, and exhausted almost to the point of death. Before I proceed, I inspect my surroundings. Rose's house looks dark and desolate, and the home on our right has lights on in the bedroom. But I don't see any movement inside. The young couple who lives there keeps to themselves, and I've always preferred it that way.

I shuffle to the entrance of the house and step on the wet porch, drenched and unable to shake myself off like a wet dog as I normally would, due to the immense pain in every inch of my body. I try not to shiver as it hurts my bones even more, but the chills on the inside of me are taking hold. For a moment I wish I could just go in and take a warm bath then snuggle under the bedcovers and sleep, but that's not why I'm here. I put my hair to the side and wipe the rain off my face as best as I can. It's so dark outside, I can barely see anything, but I know my house so well. I could walk and find things blindfolded if need be.

I approach the window, which is at the eye level, cup my face with my hands and look through it. The living room is dark except for the TV. That's one thing I never liked about this place until now. Passersby can see us, but it comes in as handy now, as I can look for Jimmy and see if he's in his usual spot. The TV projects enough light into the room that I can see everything. Jimmy is definitely there. He's sleeping on the couch, his back turned to the TV. Placing my ear against the window, I listen for any sounds, but the rain is too loud to hear anything from inside.

I walk to the door and place my hand on the doorknob, and slide it to the left. The front door is unlocked. Of course, it is. Jimmy's habit is to not lock doors at night. I've told him so many times to keep them locked, but he never listens. He keeps telling me I'm paranoid and no one would ever break into our home, for two reasons. One, the location is safe. Two, there's nothing to steal from a poor man's house. But I call the unlocked door a serendipity tonight because my house keys are sitting on the desk of my hotel room.

Before I enter, my eyes dart to the ceiling, and I notice the camera is definitely missing. Lightning strikes in the near distance, and it makes me jump. The town experiences a moment of light before quickly descending into darkness. Maybe that brief moment was enough for someone to see me sneaking into my house like a burglar, but I push away those thoughts as soon as they come.

The door opens slowly after a gentle push. As I enter, the TV blares in my ears. A soap opera is on, a stark difference from true crime shows Jimmy usually loves to dive into. A bunch of beer bottles are spread out on the table, and a nearly empty vodka bottle sits on the floor. It looks like he drank more heavily than usual today.

Jimmy isn't moving. His back changes colors as the soap opera advances into different scenes and projects light on him. His stillness is reassuring. I take the risk and creep painfully to my room to put on a different top. The soaked garment is weighing heavily on me, and makes me shiver. The view of my room makes me gasp as I enter. It looks like someone set off a bomb in there. Jimmy must have been looking for something and turned every object upside down, taken everything from the drawers of the small dresser and bedside stands. I unearth a shirt from a pile, a wreckage caused by the madman, and head back to the living room.

On my way, I tiptoe to the kitchen, certain that no quiet movement will wake him up. Just as I arrive in the kitchen, the lightning strikes again and brightens the space. A clap of thunder roars and I pray it won't wake him up. I feel the cast iron pan at my fingertips, and I grab it and turn around. I then shuffle to the living room, where Jimmy grunts and his body convulses as if he is fighting an animal. It lasts for a few seconds, but it feels like an eternity. Then it stops. He's in a tranquil state again.

The tables have turned and I'm now the one standing above him, as he has loomed over me so many times before. I put the cast iron pan overhead, then swing it as hard as I can, hitting Jimmy's head. He instantaneously wakes up, but has no time to react. He looks at me for a second with bulging eyes and an open mouth. His face is ridden with surprise, shock, and primal fear. He looks like he's about to say something, but he's unable. Because I swing the cast iron once again and hit him on the head with a dull thump. I keep hitting him, again and again, until his brain splashes all over the couch.

I drop the cast iron to the floor, and it produces a loud thud, making me jump and pulling me out of my reverie. In a flash, I see the aftermath of what I've done. The soap opera still projects the light of different colors, but all I see is red.

My eyes widen in terror.

I scream.

CHAPTER 35

A PREMEDITATED MURDER. That's what I just committed. I feel no remorse, and that scares me. Who have I become? A victim. A survivor. A murderer?

Even if a flicker of guilt emerges, I squash it by reminding myself that Jimmy would have gotten me before I got him. It's a fair game. But now I need to think of my next steps. I've got so much to do before I die. First, I still need to find my son's grave, then I need to order a gravestone, then I need to pick a charity to give all my money to.

I've been researching charities tirelessly, driven by a need to find the perfect one to receive my fortune. Then, I stumble upon a unique cause, one that resonates deeply within me - a sanctuary for drug addicts and the women who have tragically lost their babies because of addiction. The plight of these individuals strikes a chord in my heart, and I'm determined to make a difference. It's not just about the money; it's about offering hope and redemption to those who have lost their way in the shadows of addiction.

The journey to select the right charity begins, as I embark on a mission that might change lives, including my own, forever.

My immediate task is ridding of Jimmy's body.

The walls seem to close in, their silence echoing with the weight of my choices. My trembling hands clutch the blood-stained object, the cast iron pan, that turned my anguish into action. A whirlwind of thoughts churn within me–the disbelief of this irreversible act, the surge of power that came with it, and the paralyzing uncertainty of what comes next. As my gaze remains fixed on Jimmy's vacant stare, a chilling realization dawns upon me: in this single moment, I have unraveled the threads of our shared history, and the abyss of the unknown looms ahead.

Jimmy's lifeless eyes bulging at the ceiling give me chills. I place my hands on his eyelids and close them gently. Blood has saturated the couch, and I'm already thinking about what to do with it, how to remove its traces. Lightning strikes, and it lights the room, giving Jimmy's face an eerie glow. I turn the lights on and put the blinds down, making sure not an atom of light can escape.

My mind races. What do I do with the body? The house is small. There's no basement or a large yard I can dig a hole in to bury him. I run to the bedroom and take a large blanket off my bed. I place it on Jimmy, his toes sticking out. I don't want to look at the chilling display of my murdered husband. He may have been a menacing monster, but the blood-soaked body is not how I wish to remember him.

I go to bed and listen to the storm pass, as the thunder and lightning move over to the other side of the ocean. Then my eyes close and I fall asleep.

In the morning, I still feel no trace of guilt or regret. Better him than me. It's amazing what a person can achieve to preserve their own life. I pull the blanket to ensure he's dead. Dried blood covers Jimmy's face, making it barely recognizable. I put the blanket back on and head through the door. I inch my way painfully down the streets and reach the hardware store, which is only a few blocks away from our house, but it feels like forever away in this shell of a body. I suspect it's only the adrenaline making this possible. After all, I should technically be under close monitoring in a firm hospital bed at this moment, not trudging through the streets to the shop.

I find what I'm looking for and head to the register to pay. Rob, the owner I've known forever, isn't there, and I feel relief. The last thing I want is for him to ask questions, wonder what I've been up to, ask about Jimmy. I stand at the register and the man behind me asks if that's all.

Four duffle bags and a tarp.

If he asks me what it's for, and I have my answer prepared. We're painting the new house we bought recently, which is half true, and we're looking to move soon. Hence the duffle bags. But, luckily, he doesn't ask. I pay with my debit card and off I go back to the house.

I lock the door behind me and triple check the lock is secured. I'm grossed out at the task ahead of me, my stomach lurching and heaving in protest, but it must be done. It's the only way. Jimmy is heavy. Well, he is heavy for my tiny, fragile body. I pull him from the couch and push him onto the floor. His dead weight makes moving him almost impossible, and I strain to get him across the floor to the kitchen. It takes nearly thirty minutes to move his body from point A to point B, a mere several feet. But it's done.

I wipe the sweat off my forehead and kneel, giving Jimmy one last push onto the tarp spread on the floor. Now that his whole body is where I want it to be. I strip him naked and inspect him, looking at the muscles he's cultivated over the years. On his chest, where he grew a list of tattoos of female names, I notice the list has grown to three: EMMA, CHERYL, LUCY...

Female name tattoos. They look like a smudge. You'd have to come really close to discern them.

I remember him starting with Lucy. Then the list grew with the other names. Once we stopped having sex, I no longer had access to the list. I once asked him what they were. He said they were imaginary names of the fancy cars he'd buy for himself if he had money. I don't know why, but those names peeved me. They didn't belong on a body, much less on my husband's body. When I could no longer see the list grow, I pushed the memory of them to one side and tried to forget. I decided Jimmy could keep daydreaming and building an arsenal of cars in his head if he wanted to.

I head to the small hallway and open up the closet where Jimmy's tools are. The chainsaw is sitting on the shelf, its nose pointed at me. I grab it, turn it on, and get to work. With both hands, I hold the chainsaw and drift it toward Jimmy's body. I aim at the part where his name tattoos are flashing at me, and I place it gently on the first name: LUCY.

Then I begin.

CHAPTER 36

I'VE DISMEMBERED Jimmy's entire body. It's the only way to fit him into the multiple duffle bags. He's looking rather gross in his new state. Disgusting. Helpless. Like a doll, chewed on and ripped apart. His arms that hit me so many times are lying on the kitchen floor next to his head, cut from his neck. The tarp is drenched in blood.

I've seen dead bodies before, first my mother's, then my father's, at their wake, but never decapitated ones. Murder is uncommon in our neighborhood. I've never witnessed one, either, and now I can say I've committed one myself. Hard to believe, but I justify myself by again remembering Jimmy's attempt to kill me. I need to focus on the important task in front of me, but first, I will lay down to take a breather and come to my senses. Cutting up a body is hard work, even for someone who isn't dying and hasn't just suffered a spinal injury. It's so depleting, both physically and mentally, and I'm convinced the only way I was able to keep going for all those hours was because of the pure adrenaline coursing through my veins. I check the clock, and it's almost eight in the morning. No wonder I'm exhausted. I've been at it since a little after three.

The murdering part on its own had been much easier than the clean-up. Who knew taking a life would be so simple? It just takes a few swings to extinguish a whole existence.

All the body parts fit into the four duffle bags. It's a relief, because it's raining again, and I don't feel like going to the store for another bag. I crunch up the tarp and slide it to the bathtub. So much blood. I let all the blood flow down the drain. I turn on the shower, power-washing the tarp and all the blood, and I'm relieved I've been able to remove the visible signs of Jimmy's murder. A few squares of Bounty and some bleach fixes the bloodstains on the kitchen floor, and I cover the sofa with a tired looking throw from the cupboard.

But now I need to dispose of him somewhere. I wrack my brain, but then I realize what better place than the vast ocean, where sharks will feast on him? Except, I don't have a boat to get to the deeper depths.

I sit in the recliner, thinking. Now that Jimmy is gone, I'm in no immediate danger. But instead of focusing on my freedom, I watch the duffel bags, mesmerized.

The door knocks. It's ten in the morning. Who could it be?

I slide out of the chair and walk to the door. Through the peephole, I see Rose looking straight at me. Her face expression changes as if she sees me, but I know she can't. I don't want to open the door. I see her reaching for the doorbell again, and the bell sound echoes through the house a second later. How long can I keep her here until she gives up?

She looks to her left, then to her right, and then again straight at me. My leg twitches and hits the door, and I cuss under my breath. Shit.

"Jimmy? Lynn?" Rose is now knocking on the door. She knows someone is on the other side, inside the house.

I don't want to face Rose, or anyone until the body is disposed. But I can no longer fake not being here. Rose takes the knob and shifts it left and right twice. I take it in my hand and stop it from moving. I unlock the door and open it wide.

"Hey, Rose." I smile.

"Lynn. Everything okay?" She does a double take. "Don't take this the wrong way, but you look awful. What have you done to your face?"

I remember the airbag, and how close to death I looked in my reflection earlier, and mumble something about taking a tumble down the steps. Silly me, always so clumsy. I'm moving at the speed of a snail after all my body's been through, and it's impossible to hide the pain, so it makes sense to tell her something.

She walks through the door without asking if it's a convenient time. I've found Rose harmless in the past, and mostly she means well, but her snooping is annoying at the best of times.

"Yeah, everything's fine. How have you been?"

Rose sits on the couch where, just a short several hours ago, Jimmy was lying dead. Thank goodness I've covered it—there was no way I'd have been able to get those stains out this quickly. I wonder if Rose will mention anything about the bleach smell or any other unusual observations of the house. Like Jimmy missing, for example.

"I've been fine." She elongates the word "fine," then leans forward, placing her hands on her knees. "I think I heard a scream coming out of your house last night. Was that you?"

The image of me smashing Jimmy's head into pieces then letting out a big, long scream flashes in front of me. That yelp was unavoidable, like when you get on a rollercoaster and the speed shocks you.

"What scream? I honestly don't remember." I shake my head slowly. "Is it possible you might have misheard it or mistaken it for thunder?"

"No. No, Lynn. I'm pretty sure I heard a scream." She leans even further forward, then says in a whisper, "It sounded scary, and you do look like you're in a lot of pain."

I shrug and say as nonchalantly as possible, "Nope. Not me." I put my hands on my hips. "Would you like something to drink? Water? Tea? We have diet soda."

"Oh, sure. Sure. That's kind of you. How about a glass of water?"

"Coming right up." I shuffle into the kitchen and exhale a long breath while leaning against the counter so not to fall. My nerves are rattling, but I exercise deep breathing to calm myself. I bow my head and in the corner of my eye, I notice a splat of blood on the floor. Shit, shit, shit. I take a piece of paper towel, wet it in the sink and run over the spot, quickly removing it.

In the living room, I hear Rose yelling out in my direction, "Have you started moving?" She must be looking at the duffle bags sitting on the floor. I take a glass out of the cabinet and fill it with water from the sink. I waddle into the living room, my face flushing with heat. There's nothing worse than a nosy fucking neighbor asking questions.

I hand her the glass, which she puts on the coffee table, and I point at the bags. "Oh, these?"

"Um-hm." Rose nods.

"I packed up some of my clothes I'd like to donate. But yes, just preparing for our move, I guess." I look at one of the duffel bags and do a double take when I think I see blood oozing from it. How is it possible? I drained the blood as best as I could before I placed the pieces into the bags.

Rose needs to leave as soon as possible before she sees it.

"That's awfully nice of you." She picks at the seam of her skirt and averts her gaze from me before looking at me again. "Maybe your clothes fit me. Do you think I could try them?"

All my blood rushes to my head. I'm dizzy and probably about to pass out. My reaction must be so visible that Rose looks at me with pity and instantly raises her hand, as if to dismiss her question. "Oh, dear. I didn't mean to upset you. I just thought it'd be good to save you a trip, that's all."

My shoulders relax and I lower myself to the recliner before I pass out. "Oh, that's awfully kind of you, Rose, but I already called the thrift store and they're expecting it to arrive soon." I'm shocked I can come up with this bullshit so quickly.

Rose looks around. "Where is Jimmy?"

"Jimmy?" I repeat. "He went to check the house one more time. Something came up during the inspection, so he wanted to look at it a bit more closely."

Rose lifts her arm and points outside. "But his car is parked in the front. How did he get there?"

Silence ensues, and I'm yet again surprised by the ease of my lies.

"It is?" I turn my head toward the door and picture Jimmy's car sitting where he left it. "That rascal. He must have taken my car then."

Rose tilts her head and narrows her eyes. "I don't think I've ever seen Jimmy drive your car. Is something wrong with his?"

Enough with the questions already!

"That would be my guess." I stand up with urgency and announce, "I'd love to keep chatting, but I've got so many things to do. I'm so sorry, Rose. Maybe we can catch up soon?"

I walk up to the front door and open it wide.

Rose stands up slowly and walks in my direction, her eyes boring into mine. She stops in front of me and comes so close to me I can feel her breath. "Lynn, I know you're hiding something. I know it. But whatever it is, your secret won't last long."

That's okay. I don't have long anyway.

I wonder what her problem is or where all that anger is coming from, but I don't give a shit, really. She storms out of the house and stomps across the pathway, giving me one more look. Her face is contorted with anger, and her hump is looking more pronounced than I remember.

I close the door and lock it. A sudden sense of fear washes over me, and I know it won't subside until the duffle bags are out of the house.

Then something clicks in my head. An idea. I know a perfect person who can help me. I take out my phone, find his phone number, and dial.

CHAPTER 37

IT'S incredible I still have his phone number stored on my phone. I've promised myself, and once to Jimmy a long time ago, I'd never call Skull again. There was no reason to. He was my only dope peddler, always reliable and forgiving when I couldn't pay my dues right away. But I'd stored his number, just in case. It offered me comfort to know it was there, like a safety harness on a parachute.

My hands shake when I hear the phone ring. Will he even remember me?

He answers the phone. "Hello?"

He sounds the same, albeit his voice more mature, more serious. More fatigued.

"Skull?"

"Speaking." I sense the confusion in his voice.

"It's Lynn," I say, still shaking. Then there's silence.

"Lynn? Lynn Miller?"

"Yes." I squint. The more nervous I feel, the brighter the light seems to my exhausted eyes. I won't blame him if he hangs up on me. Last time I saw him was at the beach over two decades ago. I was just about to clutch the bag out of his hands when Jimmy showed up out of nowhere, walking fast in our direction, his face twisted in anger. He came up to Skull and put his face in his, threatening to kill him if he bothered me again. Skull didn't bother me, but who could ever convince Jimmy of anything?

I haven't spoken with Skull since.

"Hey, Lynn. Nice to hear from you, girl." His voice softens.

I sigh in relief. "I know I haven't talked to you in a while, but—"

"Hey, no worries. I know what married life is like. Things change, ya know. You gotta be good to your man. Be loyal and all that shit."

"About that," I stutter. "It's about Jimmy. I need you to come over and help me with something."

"Yeah, yeah. Give me a couple of hours. I just woke up. Where do you live?"

"Same place," I say and think to myself how awful that sounds.

Skull has stopped by my house so many times before, so he remembers where that is. "I'll see you shortly."

True to his words, Skull shows up at my door two hours later, looking apprehensive and smiling at the same time. I shake from the cocktail of emotions and overwhelming nostalgia, and run into his embrace. He places his hands on the small of my back and inhales deeply. "Lynn. Good to see you, girl."

Skull hasn't changed much. Well, he has gotten older, but his facial features remain soft and unassuming. He got the nickname Skull because his head is shaped just like one. He is bald and clean shaven, but there's something different about him. He looks like there's a dark cloud hanging over him, as if he's holding onto the last patches of blue sky to survive. It must be all those years of drug dealing that sometimes got him in trouble, jailed, or nearly killed. I sure am glad he is still among the living.

I first met him when I was in my early twenties. I was still a young girl with lost ambitions, and Skull looked after me, like an older brother. He'd found me behind the restaurant, lying on the ground lifeless after I nearly overdosed. He'd driven me to the hospital twice, and it was thanks to him my life had been saved more than once. I still feel connected to him even after all these years, although I don't even know his real name.

"Skull." I whisper, barely containing my happiness and relief. I feel an unexplained comfort around him. "It's so good to see you."

He enters the house and stands near the door, as if waiting to be invited inside. I imagine he might fear that Jimmy is about to show up out of nowhere and strike.

"Come on in," I say reassuringly.

His movements are stiff as he walks across the room. I invite him to sit down in the living room or the kitchen—wherever he wants. He walks into the kitchen and looks around. I wonder if he's thinking what I'm thinking: this place is a shithole, and it smells of death and bleach.

We sit at the kitchen nook, lost for words. Skull gives me a tentative smile, waiting for me to explain why I've summoned him.

"What's up, Lynn girl? You've lost some weight since I last saw you." He looks at my bosom and then back at my eyes. "But you still look hot as hell." He laughs.

I don't tell him I'm dying; it's the last thing on my mind since I killed Jimmy. At the forefront is my only wish: to get rid of his body and never see him again.

"It's Jimmy," I declare.

Skull stitches his brows together. "What about Jimmy?"

"He tried to kill me yesterday."

His eyes bulge in shock. "What? How?"

"He tampered with my car brakes. I'm sure of it. I was driving down the interstate to the cemetery..." I pause and choke up, holding back my tears. When I compose myself, I continue, "suddenly, the brakes stop working and I smash into a car in the opposite direction. I almost died."

"Shit," Skull says. "Where is he now?"

"That's why you're here, Skull." I bow my head and search for the right words to tell him. I look up and stare Skull in the eyes. "I killed him."

"Whoa, whoa," Skull says. His eyes are enormous in his small head, and I can tell his mind is racing. "Where is he?"

I point my index finger toward the living room. "Over there. I put him in the duffel bags."

"You did what?" Skull's eyes are etched in shock. He

leans back on the seat and runs his hand across his forehead, even though there's no speck of sweat on it.

"Take a look if you want."

He stares at me, as if considering this option, then stands up and walks to the duffel bags. I hear the zipper slide and seconds later, Skull gags and runs to the bathroom. He retches in the toilet, and the sound reverberating through the house is nauseating.

He returns to the kitchen, wiping his mouth. His face is as white as the paper towels sitting on the countertop.

"Are you okay?"

"Shit, girl. I didn't know you had it in you."

"Me neither. But I had to. I'm pretty sure he was going to kill me."

He nods, as if he understands. "I've seen dead bodies, but nothing like this before. It's … it's sickening."

"I know." I bow my head in embarrassment. Panic had taken over, and I couldn't think straight to come up with a better plan to dispose of his body. This was probably a huge mistake.

"What do you want me to do with the bags?" he manages eventually.

"Toss them in the ocean. If you know anyone who has a boat, it would be best to find a deep spot."

"I think I know a few people who can help. That won't be a problem," he says. "You know, this will cost you, Lynn."

"How much?"

He looks around the kitchen and probably wonders what I can afford. "It will be a 100k."

"Okay."

He gives me a surprising grimace, then wipes his face with his finger. "Wow."

"I won the lottery a couple of weeks ago. Five million. Everything started shortly after I won it. A woman started to follow me around, and I think she conspired with Jimmy against me. I still don't know what to do about her—"

I stop suddenly and shake my head. "The lottery is to blame for everything. My life went from bad to worse."

Skull tilts his head while listening. He straightens his head and says, "I'm here for you if you need anything else. For that..." he points his arm toward the living room... "I'll come around two this morning and get the bags. You don't need to worry a thing."

"Excellent. I'll have money ready."

Skull gets up and heads for the door. Before he exits, he turns around and opens his arms wide. I walk into his embrace while exhaling. He squeezes me twice and I muster, "Thank you. Thank you, my friend."

The tension inside me has significantly lowered now that Jimmy, my tormentor, is gone. It's like fog has been peeled away, and now I can see.

I sit in the recliner, and for the first time, I feel renewed. A small smile forms on my face. No more beatings, no more being controlled, no more constant fear of the next turn. When people aren't under constant control and pressure, they have more room and time to think.

I stare at the duffle bags sitting on the floor, and just like the contents inside, the thought that crosses my mind is vile and corpulent. It's a thought I haven't had before, but as soon as it pops into my head, nausea overwhelms me, and I want to run to the bathroom and retch. It's the realization I haven't grappled with until now—now that I have so much time and freedom to think, it's all coming back to me. I will need to deal with it on Earth, otherwise I will be in hell in just a few short weeks.

The thought that won't leave me alone is about my whole nuclear family—and how they're dead because of me.

CHAPTER 38

BACK TO THE dreadful year 1997.

The room is cast in a subdued glow, the warm light of a lone lamp on the nightstand carving out a small pocket of comfort amid the encroaching darkness. I perch on the edge of the bed, my body weighed down by the burden of my secret. My fingers tremble as they brush against my distended belly, the evidence of my hidden transgressions.

In my hand, I hold a tiny bag, its contents a lifeline I have clung to for months. The room is quiet, the only sound the soft hum of the air conditioner, a stark contrast to the turmoil raging within me.

The bag feels cool against my clammy skin as I turn it over and over, a ritualistic dance of anxiety and desperation. My lips move in a whisper, the words a fragile mantra to steel my resolve.

"Just one more time. Just one more time, and then I can stop using."

Gathering my strength, I try to stand, my hands

seeking the steadying support of the nightstand. The sixth month of my pregnancy has turned my once graceful movements into stumbling uncertainty. I sway precariously, my heart echoing in my ears before regaining my balance.

"I can't let him find out," I whisper to myself, my voice cracking with the weight of my deceit.

As if summoned by fate, the bedroom door creaks open, and Jimmy enters the room, his brows furrowed with concern and a tinge of frustration. His eyes fall upon me, a mix of worry and puzzlement playing across his features.

"Lynn," he begins, "we need to talk."

"What about?"

His sigh echoes through the room. He locks his eyes onto me, and I try my best to conceal my fear.

"You've been distant and secretive," he says. "I don't know what's going on with you, but I want us to work through it."

I force a smile and place my hand on his cheek. "There's nothing to worry about. I'm not hiding anything. I promise. It's just … the pregnancy has been overwhelming and I don't want to burden you."

Jimmy's gaze softens, his concern mingling with a compassion that sends shivers down my spine. I am a complete and utter fraud. He reaches out, his hand cupping my cheek as if trying to protect me.

"Okay, baby-face," he concedes. "But we're in this together, remember?"

I nod. "Absolutely," I say, even though I know it's a far cry from the truth.

I am a liar. Days pass, and nothing changes. Absolutely nothing.

The next day, I find myself home alone. Again. The room is dimly lit, with shadows playing eerie games on the walls. An air of desperation hangs heavy, suffocating the silence. In the center of the room, I'm sprawled out on the floor, my breaths shallow and irregular. Unbeknownst to anyone, I carry a secret burden within me, one that intensifies the gravity of the situation.

I have succumbed to the temptation of a dark escape. My mind now swirls in a haze of confusion and guilt, trapped in a waking nightmare of my making. As the minutes pass, I feel the weight of my actions closing in around me, a sinister reckoning approaching.

Just when the world around me seems to fade into a chilling oblivion, the creaking of the front door startles my senses awake. A surge of hope arrives. Through the haze, I see the silhouette of a man stepping into the dimly lit room. It's Jimmy, an expected twist of fate that will soon prove to be my salvation.

Worry etches across my husband's face as he rushes to my side. I think I can hear him cuss out, but he continues to focus on reviving me, as he notices my pale complexion and labored breathing. He runs to the landline phone, hastily dialing the emergency number, hoping they will arrive in time. On his way back, he grabs a kitchen towel and wets it, kneeling to my side and places the towel on my forehead. Next, he quickly slaps my face and calls my name in panic, begging me to stay awake.

As the ambulance sirens pierce through the night, my consciousness drifts in and out like an elusive dream. I vaguely register Jimmy's words, his voice urging me to stay awake. I try to speak, to apologize for the choices that have led me to this terrifying moment, but my words are lost in a sea of confusion.

The paramedics arrive, their faces masked in professionalism, but their eyes betraying compassion. They quickly assess my condition, their attention heightened by the realization of my pregnancy. With a gentle yet urgent touch, they place me on a stretcher and rush me out of the shadowed room into the harsh glare of ambulance lights.

Jimmy sits beside me, looking torn between guilt for not having been there sooner and relief that he found me when he did. I don't think I need to remind him I've escaped from death before. Fear and concern mingle in his eyes, as if he's thinking about the gravity of the situation and the precious life at stake. The life I carry inside—our unborn son.

En route to the hospital, my mind continues to drift between consciousness and the abyss. The town lights blur outside the ambulance windows, a surreal backdrop to the turmoil within. My thoughts are a tangled web of regrets, fears, and the hope of a second—third, fourth—chance.

As the ambulance speeds through the night, Jimmy's unwavering presence provides a faint glimmer of hope.

Amid my disorientation and pain, I clung to his support like a lifeline, finding solace in knowing that he found us.

The hospital doors swing open, and the flurry of medical professionals surrounds me, ushering me into the sterile, yet life-saving environment. Jimmy stays close, unwilling to leave my side. As the doctors work urgently to stabilize me, he whispers words of encouragement, promising to be there no matter what.

In this critical moment, a haunting realization dawns on me—the life I carry is not just my burden, but also my reason to fight. With newfound determination, albeit maybe too late, I vow to embrace another chance I've been given, to confront my demons, and to find redemption for myself and my unborn child. The road ahead will be challenging. But winning the fight is my only option.

My eyes roll in my sockets and the next thing I know, I've fallen into a dark oblivion.

CHAPTER 39

I WAS WELL aware of the potential harm that drug use could inflict on my baby. Each time I consumed heroin, I understood that it diminished my child's chances of survival. I kept it a secret from Jimmy that I had been neglecting my doctor's appointments. The recommended schedule was to attend these appointments every two months for ultrasound scans to monitor the baby's growth and development. During these visits, the doctor routinely assessed my blood pressure, weight, and drew blood. The thought of my addiction being discovered through these blood tests was a constant concern, and the risk associated with such exposure was simply too great.

In retrospect, my actions were incredibly self-centered. I prioritized my own needs over the well-being of my child.

My thoughts are consumed by the state of my life. By what I have become. A murderer. Drugs killed my child, but now only drugs can give me relief, a reprieve from the pain.

I dial Skull an hour after he'd left. "Please bring the goods over tonight."

"Are you sure?" he says. He sounds like the brother I've never had. "You've been clean for years. You want to go down that rabbit hole again?"

"It's okay." Maybe it's my chance to tell him about the cancer, but I still can't get the words out of my mouth. I want to explain to him it doesn't matter anymore. Now that I have little time to live, I'm trying to undo things done and do things undone.

I still have a lot to do before death consumes me. Finding my son's grave is going to be a challenge, but I'm determined. Aren't there groundskeepers in the graveyards I can ask? There has to be a way. I'm also close to picking a charity of my liking. Things are coming together. I'm achieving some clarity even though my life is riddled with muddled pain.

This reminds me. I have to call Cecilia and cancel our offer on the house. If she asks why, I'll tell her another opportunity came along. Outside of Hampton. Far from here. Far from awful memories.

I take my phone and dial, but Cecilia doesn't pick up. I hang up without leaving a message. It's not the way to communicate such an important matter. I dial her office number. No one answers. Her unavailability gives me the feeling of unease, but I try not to dwell on it.

I call her cell phone again, only to be greeted by her voicemail message: This is Cecilia Smith. Please leave a message and I will get back to you as soon as I can.

"Hi, Cecilia. This is Lynn Miller. I need to speak with you about the property my husband James and I put an offer on. Can you call me back? Please."

I hang up and feel better that I'm making at least some progress toward my goals. I admit living in that house would be grand, but there's no point in enjoying it for mere days.

I've been cursed and nothing works to my advantage. Absolutely nothing. But I'm looking forward to Skull's delivery.

When he arrives at two in the morning, he is discrete and quiet. I open the door for him, but he doesn't even look at me. He marches into the house and goes for the bags. In the car, a man sits in the passenger seat. It's so dark outside, I can only see the silhouette through the window. I'm assuming this is his guy with a boat, the one who will take Jimmy hundreds of feet from the shore and drop him into the water like a useless pile of rocks. Jimmy had joked once or twice he wanted to be "buried" in the ocean. *Hey, just throw me in there, and all will be good.* I questioned his sanity back then, but now I question only mine.

Skull comes back for the other two bags. Before he takes them in his hands, he pulls a bag out of his pocket and puts it on the table. "Just be careful, okay?"

I tell him I'll wire him the money, as soon as today, and he nods with a smile. He takes the bag handles and walks out.

The house suddenly feels empty and eerie. Even though the physical parts of Jimmy are gone, the traces of him are everywhere: the recliner, the couch, the kitchen. I can hear his voice echoing between the walls, even though they are just the remnants of memories in my head. I'd like to escape them, and perhaps I should stay at the hotel for the rest of my time, but something strange pulls me into this house I've always called home. For better or for worse.

I am a murderer, and that's what murderers do. They get tied to the scene of murder. They relive the demise. They drink it in.

I shake my head, struggling to rid those thoughts.

I take the bag from the coffee table and head to the bedroom. There, I lie down and take all the contents out of the bag. It feels as if no time has passed. When the drugs enter my veins, I instantly enter a different world. A better kind. A carefree kind. I close my eyes as I flow into the air. Pictures of my son flash in front of my eyes, and I extend my arm to hold him for the first time. I tell him I'll see him soon. We have a full and beautiful conversation. I beg him for forgiveness, for mercy, and I promise I will do better in the afterlife.

But then he screams at me. He calls me a murderer and tells me I belong in hell and will never be atoned.

CHAPTER 40

NOTHING GOOD COMES out of murder.

Deep down, I know that, but in my mind, I justify killing Jimmy. It was in self-defense. But the guilt has multiplied, regardless. I've erased my whole family. What shitty person in their right mind does that? Clearly, I'm not in a rational state of mind. I haven't been myself lately. Ever since I won the lottery. I've heard people say money messes with your mind, and I'm starting to think it's true. I'm a victim of it.

I'm not surprised that I'm being haunted in my dreams. My nightmares are vivid, and they remind me of who I have become.

If I give away all my lottery money for a good cause, maybe my guilt will erase like sand on the beach as a tide rises. Maybe I can find redemption and die in peace. All the possibilities. And that reminds me to call the chosen foundation soon and tell them about my donation. I've got so much to do, and I'm feeling lethargic and overwhelmed, unable to make my first move. It doesn't help that my health worsens every day, and every bone in my body is slowly giving up on me.

I have never had time to mourn the loss of my child. It's because Jimmy took me under his control spell. He beat me whenever I did anything he would disapprove of. But now that he's gone, I'm back to feeling what I'm supposed to feel: grief. I wipe my tears and whisper a mantra to myself: "Be strong. Be strong. Be strong."

As I pull the contents out of the bag for another dose, the doorbell sounds. I inch myself slowly out of bed and peek through the bedroom window. A cop is standing on my porch, his right hand resting on the pistol sitting on his hip. He's looking around in every direction, and I can now see his full face. It's Danny, the cop who'd showed up at my accident the other day.

I fix my hair quickly and put a cardigan on, even though the heat in the house is unbearable. My stabbed arm is the last thing I want Danny to see. I approach the door and open it slowly, shaking from the unexpected visit. Does he know I've killed Jimmy? If he does, I am ready to surrender. I probably deserve whatever it is I should be punished with.

Danny stands on my porch, looking through the hole where a plank is missing. At the sound of the door creaking, he lifts his head and looks at me.

"Hey, Lynn."
"Danny?"

His eyebrows stitch together, as if he seems surprised to see me.

"May I come in?"

I open the door wide and let him in.

"Yes, come in."

Danny steps into the house and makes a face, like he smells something vile inside. He looks around, then his gaze lands on me. "Aren't you supposed to be in the hospital?"

The hospital staff had said I should stay there at least a week. But since I'd successfully escaped, no one has looked for me. If Danny thinks I should be in the hospital, then what is he doing turning up at my doorstep?

"I was too busy to stay."

"Too busy to get better? Nonsense!"

I give him a small smile.

As I close the door and turn around, I watch Danny walk across the living room and into the kitchen. He peeks his head into the bedroom, then the bathroom and comes back into the living room where I'm standing, now sweating from wearing the cardigan.

"What can I do for you?" I ask.

"Are you alone?"

I nod quickly. "Yes. Yes, I am."

"May I sit?" He looks at the couch and walks over to it before I can answer. He sits down on the spot where just recently I beat Jimmy to death with the cast iron. His blood is still covering the couch, and only a thin throw blanket separates it from Danny's butt. He's probably here to investigate his disappearance. I highly doubt that Skull or his men have said anything. Skull is professional and loyal, and I've paid him enough to do the deed and keep his mouth shut. Perhaps someone caught them. Maybe someone having a sleepless night was hanging by the shore and saw a strange movement on the surface in a distance, hands dropping duffel bags into the depth of the ocean. And if all this got to the police, then wow. I'm impressed with the speed at which they connected all that action to his disappearance.

I sit in the recliner, swallowing the lump in my throat. The best thing is to stay calm and be honest and truthful. I wait for him to ask me questions.

"I'm here to check in on you. The hospital called reporting your escape. I want to make sure you're alright."

I nod and sigh in relief. Perhaps Danny's visit has nothing to do with Jimmy. "Yeah, I'm fine. I didn't have a chance to talk to my doctor or nurse before I took off." I shrug and give a small smile.

Danny nods. "I don't think they would have advised you to up and go like that. Especially since you'd just got into a serious accident."

He leans forward, his elbows sitting on his lap, and his eyes boring into me. I'm assuming this is all Danny came here for, but his next question makes me break into sweat, and I don't think it's the cardigan this time.

"Your husband is here?" he begins. Danny is one of those cops Jimmy has known for ages, I remind myself again. They're not friends, but they could pass for being buddies, exchanging favors when necessary.

I shake my head.

"You make sure he takes care of you."

"I will." That wouldn't happen in a million years, even if Jimmy was alive.

Then Danny says something that is completely out of place, incongruent with everything I have ever believed. "Jimmy is a good guy. I know he will."

Maybe Danny knows something I don't.

I nod.

"So, listen, your car has been inspected after the accident." I flinch at his words. "Something has chewed on your brakes, causing them to be loose. The mechanic says it's most likely a rat."

My eyes widen. "Are you sure? A rat?"

I begin to tremble, and my stomach roils. Rats are common in the parking lots of hotels, even fancy ones, thanks to amount of food they dispose of, so that's easy to believe. But if it's true—if rats were to blame for the accident—it means I was wrong. Have I killed Jimmy for nothing?

No, not nothing, my mind whispers. He still beat the shit out of me over and over.

This sonofabitch, Danny. He is staring me right in the eye, not even a small twitch, and lying right to my face. Rats? Chewing on brakes? What idiot would I need to be to believe the horseshit he's spewing out? There's no goddamn way rats would inhabit the proximity of the fanciest hotel in town.

I get it. It's all a cover up.

I'm going to be sick. I need Danny to leave.

"Are you okay?" Danny asks.

I unclench the recliner sides, realizing how tight I've been gripping them.

"Yes."

Danny looks around again and says. "Anyway, where is Jimmy?"

"I don't know where he is. We've been fighting a lot since I won the lottery. We can't seem to agree what to do with the money. So, he leaves the house for indefinite amounts of time, but I don't know where he goes. He comes home eventually." The words keep running out of my mouth at top speed.

I look at him straight in the eye, hoping to convey truth. My version of it, anyway.

"I see. Well, when he comes back, tell him to take care of you."

He stands up and heads for the door. I follow slowly, every step I take causing me agony. "You know he will."

"I hope you feel better from the accident."

"Thank you."

As soon as Danny leaves, I run to the bedroom and get another dose. It's the only way to deal with the pain.

CHAPTER 41

NOW THAT I have a newfound freedom and am no longer under Jimmy's spell, I can do whatever I want. I can do my best to escape reality, for at least just a short amount of time. I decide it's time to revisit the forgotten hobbies, pleasures, and activities.

One evening, I stroll down to my old stomping ground, the only casino in town I used to visit all the time until Jimmy forbade me to go. The establishment from the outside looks the same, except for the paint job of the external wall. It used to be dark brown, and now the walls are white, looking more inviting. The sign appended on the roof by large metal poles remains the same. HAMPTON CASINO. Its red plastic letters are enormous, and you can't miss them.

I'd be here regularly once upon a time. My favorite games were blackjack and poker, and I'd spend hours here, gambling my money away. I'd win once in a while, making a small profit, but casinos aren't meant to make you rich, so most of my bets ended up wasted. But what I appreciated about the place was that every employee knew me. I'd enter and they would greet me by the name, a cheer roaring across the floor.

Today is different. When I set foot inside, the employees barely notice me. I don't look like someone with money. I have millions in my checking account, but I haven't upgraded my wardrobe, much less gone to a hair or nail salon to get a fix. Nothing to make me look better. Healthier. Maybe it hasn't fully registered with my brain that I can improve my life by a lot, but then why would it? I have so little time.

Hesitantly, I move forward, pushing away the old memories. Nothing will be the same again, nor should I expect it to be. The low hum of conversation and the clinking of chips against the tables form an eerie backdrop to the scene, setting the stage for what could become a night I'll never forget.

My heart pounds in my chest as I approach the blackjack table, my eyes scanning the room like a hawk searching for prey. Weeks of paranoia have led me here, to this moment of reckoning. I can't shake the feeling that someone has been following me, lurking in the shadows, always just out of sight. I question if that young woman is still after me now that Jimmy is gone.

The dealer shuffles the cards with a practiced rhythm, and the atmosphere in the casino is a heady mix of excitement and anxiety.

As I place my bet and receive my first two cards, I find

myself momentarily lost in the simple yet intoxicating world of the game. The cards feel cool and smooth in my hands. I place my chosen card on the table, then I watch the dealer reveal his face-up card—an eight of hearts. My heart races once more, but this time, it is the thrill of the game that consumes me. It's been so long, and I barely contain my excitement.

I glance at the other players at the table, a diverse group of individuals with their own reasons for being there. Some are focused and intent, while others chat nervously, attempting to mask their anxiety with forced laughter. The woman across from me has a confident, almost predatory air about her, making me wonder if she is a regular or simply another soul seeking escape from reality. Like me.

The dealer's voice breaks through my thoughts as she turns over her down card to reveal a five of spades. The tension in the air grows palpable, and the weight of my decisions presses down on me. Should I hit, hoping to get closer to twenty-one? Or should I stay, not risking going over and busting? I used to be so good at this. Led by some luck, but mostly instinct.

I decide to hit, my fingers trembling as I accept another card—a three of diamonds. I'm now at twelve, far from the safety of twenty-one. The risk is real, and my every instinct tells me to stay, but something inside me pushes for one more card.

With a deep breath, I signal for another hit, and the dealer hands me a seven of clubs. I am now at nineteen, a high-risk move, but just two points away from blackjack. My heart pounds in my chest as I watch the dealer reveal her down card—a two of spades. She has seventeen, a vulnerable position.

The casino seems to hold its breath as she draws another card—an eight of diamonds. Bust. The collective sigh of relief and elation from the table is almost deafening.

I win. Luck has served me well lately, albeit too late.

As the stares around the table bore into me, I freeze, noticing a familiar figure sitting at another blackjack table across from mine. A figure, slender, with long, flowing black hair that cascades like a waterfall down her back. It's her, the woman who has been haunting my every step, my every thought. My breath catches in my throat as I watch her from a close distance, my grip on the edge of the blackjack table tightening.

Summoning every ounce of courage, I push myself forward, determined to confront her. The adrenaline coursing through my veins makes my every step feel like a herculean effort. My heart beats hard as I approach the figure, my mind racing with all the questions I'd been dying to ask.

As I reach out to tap her shoulder, my fingers brush against the dark, silken strands of her hair, sending shivers down my spine. The figure turns, slowly revealing the face, and my heart sinks like a stone. It isn't her. It is a man, a stranger, with an expression of confusion and irritation.

"Sorry, I thought you were someone else," I stammer, my voice barely above a whisper.

He gives me a quizzical look, then turns away without a word, clearly uninterested in my explanation. My face flushes with embarrassment as I retreat, feeling the eyes of the casino patrons on me, judging, mocking.

I slump back into my chair at the blackjack table, my hands trembling. My stalker has eluded me once again, blending into the chaos of the casino, leaving me to question my sanity. The maze of paranoia and fear in my mind has never felt more suffocating, and I realize that the true terror lies not in the woman who may or may not have been following me but in the paranoia that had taken root within me, twisting my perception of reality into a nightmare.

I crawl out of the chair and shuffle away, leaving my winning behind.

CHAPTER 42

A PHONE IS BUZZING NEARBY, but I can't locate it right away. It's definitely on mute, as it's vibrating constantly. It must be Jimmy's phone, and the sound seems to come from the couch. I approach the couch and follow the buzzing sound until I come closer. Under the blanket, I find his iPhone tucked between the couch cushions. Jimmy didn't like phones much; he used them only when he needed them.

A call from a woman named Anna is coming through. Who is Anna? Jimmy never mentioned her name, as far as I can recall. I'm tempted to pick up the phone and ask who she is, but I expect an awkward conversation when she hears my voice instead of Jimmy's, and then how would I explain where Jimmy is? I ignore her call and it goes to voicemail. She seems to be persistent, and she calls again, but I don't pick up.

Seconds later, a text comes through from Anna. I can

read the first line without opening his password-protected phone and read: *my attorney sent you a letter two days ago.*

An attorney? Was Jimmy in big trouble, being chased by authorities? Danny was just here; wouldn't he have said something if that were the case? The curiosity gets the better of me, and I look for the letter. What does it contain? Is Anna a long-lost cousin after our lottery money? I hope not.

I look around the house to find a letter addressed to Jimmy. We have never received much mail except for utility bills and junk. Jimmy used to have subscription to car magazines, but he canceled them all to save money. I look for the usual places we leave our mail—under the coffee table, the kitchen counter, sprawled around the house on the floor—but the letter is nowhere to be found. Maybe it's still sitting in our mailbox in the front.

I storm out of the door, and the second I set foot outside, I regret the timing. Rose is mowing her front lawn and sees me when she turns around. I want to run for the hills and hide in the house, but it's too late. Rose has already seen me and turns off her lawn mower before waving in my direction.

Rose always shows up at the wrong place and at the wrong time. Or perhaps I do.

"Hey, Lynn."

I stroll down the stairs and across my front yard and stop to have a word with Rose. "Hey."

"Nice day to mow the lawn. But it looks like it's going to rain." She looks up and so do I, but all I see is the vast blue sky and not one cloud. "Okay, maybe not today."

Her small talk infuriates me, especially when I have important things to do.

"Yeah, I don't think so, Rose." I inch toward the mailbox and try to ignore her, but she persists.

"So, are you all set to move?"

"Not yet."

She snaps her head back and purses her lips. "Really?"

"Yes, why is that so surprising?" I can't hide my annoyance.

"Well, I guess it's not. Especially since Jimmy is still away, right?" She bulges her eyes at me and eagerly awaits my answer.

"You got it, Rose. Now, if you will excuse me, I have things to do."

"What is it with you, Lynn? You're always so busy, always running around. Ever since you won the lottery, you seem a little ... frazzled. Are you okay?"

"I'm fine, Rose. I'm trying to get my business in order before I move, that's all."

By now, I hope Cecilia has gotten my voicemail and will call me shortly, so I can cancel the offer.

I open the mailbox and peer inside to see a Stop & Shop catalogue and an envelope perched inside. Our address on the envelope is handwritten and addressed to Jimmy. It must be the letter this Anna person mentioned in her text. My body shivers with nerves, and I stare at it, dying to tear it open.

"I see. Well, let me know if you need anything." Rose disrupts my concentration.

I look up and see Rose pulling the string on her mower, ready to continue on with her chore. "I will."

The lawn-mower's engine revs and I storm into the house. I sit in the recliner and stare at the envelope. I don't recognize the handwriting. I open it, and inside is a single sheet piece of A4 paper, folded in three. With trembling hands, I open the letter, my heart racing from the storm of emotions that grip me. The words inked on the paper shimmer, cruel in their starkness.

Dear Mr. James Corrigan:

We hope this letter finds you well. We are writing to inform you that a paternity test has confirmed your biological connection to our client's child, Emma.

I gasp in shock, my breath caught in my throat. My eyes dart across the page, grappling with each sentence as it unfolds. I continue reading:

I understand that circumstances change, and our focus should always be on what is best for the child. With this in mind, I kindly request your financial support in the form of child alimony.

This support will ensure that Emma has access to opportunities and resources she deserves as she grows.

I am committed to fostering a healthy co-parenting relationship for the sake of Emma's happiness and stability. I believe that by working together in a respectful and collaborative manner, we can ensure that she has the best possible future.

Enclosed with this letter, you will find a breakdown of estimated costs for Emma's well-being, including education, healthcare, and general expenses. I urge you to consider the significance of your role in her life and the positive impact your support can make.

I am open to discussing the details of child alimony and exploring a fair arrangement that aligns with your financial circumstances. Please feel free to reach out to me to initiate the dialogue about this matter.

Your contribution will play a vital role in shaping Emma's life, and I trust that you will do what is right for her. Thank you for taking the time to read this letter. I look forward to hearing from you and finding a resolution that benefits Emma's well-being.

Sincerely,
Robert Schuster, Esq.

I drop the letter to my lap and deeply exhale. Anna seeks alimony for their child, a child borne of Jimmy's extramarital affair. My mind is churning, each word a weight upon my conscience, each revelation a cut that runs deep.

The circumstances, the demands, the implications, they formed a mosaic of betrayal, a distorted portrait of a man I believed I knew so well. My mind races through memories, moments that suddenly make sense—arriving home late, anger and violence, the tattoos. EMMA, CHERYL, LUCY. All the names Jimmy plastered on his body as a tattoo. Now I wonder if these are his children's names, and not imaginary cars like he led me to believe.

I close my eyes, as if shutting out the world for a moment. My breaths come ragged, a storm raging within me as I grapple with the enormity of what I've just discovered. A tear slips down my cheek, mingling with the turmoil that churns inside me.

But the irony isn't lost on me–this letter, the very thing that could catalyze the ultimate downfall of our marriage, lay before me as a testament to the life I have ended. With trembling hands, I fold the letter, the paper whispering secrets as it crinkles under my touch.

The world closes in on me. I've killed a child's father.

I can't breathe.

CHAPTER 43

LIKE A WILD ANIMAL that's just released from its cage, I hobble straight for the door. The house is too claustrophobic and I can't stand the thought of spending another moment inside. I find myself on my front lawn, hyperventilating, taking deep breaths. I close my eyes for a second, and like a magnet pulling me in, I go through the open gate and head to town.

Rose is standing in her yard, but I'm too distracted to notice her. My legs are moving with no thought given to the movement. Rose is watching me at the periphery of her garden, perplexed, extending her arms toward me.

"Lynn, Lynn, are you okay?"

Her voice is deep with concern. She says something else, but I tune her voice out. She's trying to stop me by catching my arm, but I bring it closer to my body and walk around her, continuing on my journey. To where, I do not know. I let my feet take me.

"Lynn! Come back! You're looking awfully sick. Lynn!"

But I don't stop. I don't respond. I keep going.

I'm in a trance.

I find myself on the main street along the beach, where a sea of people is walking in both directions. The ocean today is unfriendly, keeping swimmers at bay. Amid surfers enjoying themselves in the ocean, Jimmy's lifeless body remains unnoticed.

Jimmy.

When I walk, I see his face attached to the bodies walking in the opposite direction. I flinch when Jimmy's eyes meet mine. My head snaps back. My eyes bulge at the faces that appear to look just like Jimmy, but when their expressions change, I realize it is not him after all.

Why are they messing with me? Why can't they just leave me alone?

Sweat is dripping down my back. As I walk among the people, I whisper Jimmy's name. My face is contorted with anger. Rage. But also agony.

I watch the people walking around me, happy in their carelessness. Am I the only one among them capable of killing an entire family? The thought sickens me, and I feel the bile rising in my esophagus.

What have I done? How could I be so selfish?

Eyes are watching me. Someone is following me. Is it the ghosts? I turn around and clearly see her. She is standing in the middle of the sea of people, staring at me. Her long dark hair, parted in the middle, covers her eyes, hiding the dark gaze. She's staring at me, standing there, lifeless, waiting for me to do something. We look at each other for a few long seconds, and I shake my head in disbelief. There's my enemy. She has found me.

I need to get away from her. I drag my feet as fast as I can move them, cursing the slowness of my broken body. I trip and fall, landing on the palms of my hands. My body has slowly given up, but I'm determined to keep going. A woman around my age comes near me and offers her hand to lift me up. I shake my head and thank her. I don't need her help.

I summon every ounce of strength to inch myself up from the ground and keep going. I quicken my steps when I see the public bathroom at one end of the beach road. Washing my face will help me come to my senses. I run inside and dive toward the sink, hyperventilating. Coughing returns and I open my mouth, only to see blood clots coming out, getting stuck at the bottom of the basin. My chest feels heavy. Dying in this bathroom is not on my to-do list, but it wouldn't be unexpected.

I bend over like that for a minute or two until I feel better. My heartbeat slows down and I can focus again. When I lift my head and look at myself in the mirror, a dark figure appears in the background.

It's her.

She is standing behind me, with her long black hair parted in the middle, her eyes deeply focused on me.

I widen my eyes in fear and, from the top of my lungs, I scream.

CHAPTER 44

I THINK I hear her voice. The word I've always wanted to hear but no one has ever addressed me with.

"Mother!"

"Stay away!" I scream, my voice full of fear and panic. I extend my arm toward the young woman as if I'm carrying a weapon. My hands are empty, but keeping her away at a distance gives me peace of mind, an inexplainable comfort.

She is slowly approaching me, and I move backwards until I hit the wall.

"Mom?" she repeats.

Her words don't register with me until I get a better look at her. As I study her, my fear melts away. Curiosity sets in instead. Who is she, and what could she possibly want? It feels like I'm looking at something familiar that was once out of reach, but is now within my grasp. Her soft eyes want to say something; she wants to connect with me.

She has an important message to convey. I don't sense an ounce of danger in her.

I catch myself in the mirror for a split second. My mouth is agape, and my jaw has dropped.

Did I hear her correctly: Mom? Why is she calling me this?

"Mother," she repeats. "My name is Lucy. I was born in the Portsmouth Regional Hospital in October, 1997. They then took me away and gave me to a family." She chokes up and looks like she's about to cry. My ears are adjusting to what she is telling me, and I cannot believe it. "You are my biological mother. I'm glad I have found you."

Instead of embracing this news, I shake my head in denial and repeat, "No. No, no, no. It's impossible. I gave birth to a baby boy, and he is dead."

She cocks her head to the side, stitches her brows in sadness, and looks at me. "They lied to you, mother. All of it."

She inches toward me slowly, as if she's taming a wild animal. As she gets closer, her facial features become more prominent. Her deep blue eyes look just like Jimmy's. Her cheek dimples resemble mine. Besides those blue eyes, she's a spitting image of me—I can finally see that clearly. When I was around her age, my stature was similar. We are the same height, nearly the same weight.

I'm starting to believe her. The information she gives me checks out. That dreadful day of October 1, 1997. The day I gave birth to a stillborn child by an emergency cesarean section. That afternoon when Jimmy came home after work, he'd found me on the bedroom floor, lifeless. I'd taken a high dose of heroin, the secret I'd kept from him during my entire pregnancy. He called 9-1-1 immediately, hoping he'd save two lives at once.

The day resurfaces out of the depth of my memory.

After I gave birth, I remember Jimmy sitting next to my hospital bed, holding my hand. I'd assumed we had a son. It was what Jimmy had wanted all along. A son he could play with, become best friends with. But I also remember no one talked about my baby, dead or alive. Not Jimmy, not the doctor, not the nurses. In retrospect, I understand why. While they tried to save one life (mine), they gave away another one. They must have thought I wasn't fit to be a mother, to care for a child when all I cared about was drugs.

I wonder if things would have been different if I'd given birth to a baby boy. Would Jimmy have ended up keeping it? Or would he have given the baby away, like he abandoned Emma? Or Cheryl?

And now I remember he wasn't overly sad about the news. He had a dead face about him that morning. He was saying he worried about me more than he worried about anything else. Then the following day, he took me home and never spoke about our child again.

Now I understand everything. Jimmy had a preference for sons and disregarded every daughter he had. Including our own.

Lucy is standing in front of me, and I give her a big

embrace, squeezing her as hard as I can manage with my frail arms. While we hold each other, I feel her body convulsing and I'm pretty sure she is crying.

I gently put my hand on the back of her head and whisper. "Don't cry, baby. I'm here. I'm here at last."

CHAPTER 45

"LET'S SIT AT THE BEACH." I'm mesmerized by the fact that my daughter, now in her mid-twenties, is standing next to me. I squeeze her hand once, twice, to make sure I'm not dreaming. Her body is all too real. Her skin under mine is so soft.

We walk toward the beach and keep looking at each other like we can't believe our eyes. Shy, reserved, shocked we have found each other. She tangles her arm in mine and smiles.

"How about we sit here?" She points at an empty spot at the beach, far from other people. We sit down, facing each other and holding hands. It's the first time someone has called me mother. The first time anyone has craved to be in my presence. I soak up all of it. I hold my daughter tightly, wishing I could have done so every day for the past twenty-five years.

"Where do we even begin?" I laugh, nervous.

She shrugs. "I don't know. Wherever you want."

Her voice is soothing. Her eyes project innocence, and all I want to do is give her a hug and never let her go.

"When I gave birth, I was told you didn't survive." I bow my head, hiding my shame. I'm not sure if I should leave out the drug abuse part, but I decide it's best I am honest with her completely. "I had some problems with drug use and your father told me the drugs were to blame for your ... passing."

She looks at me with eyes wide open. I hope she won't judge me. But I wouldn't blame her if she did.

"I'm so sorry." Tears come out of my eyes involuntarily.

She takes my hand and kisses it. "It's okay, Mom. I've had a happy life. A kind and generous couple adopted me."

A pang of jealousy goes through me, even though I'm happy she has had a decent life. I want to know all about her adopted family, but it's better to wait and ask the questions later. All I want to do now is savor her presence, study her face, feel her skin. Love her for the very first time.

"I'm glad to hear you've had a decent life."

"Only a few years ago, I asked them to tell me who my biological parents were, and they told me. They also told me you were dead—and that you've been dead for as long as I've been alive. That you died when you delivered me." She smiles. "Isn't it ironic? We both thought the other was dead."

"I wish I hadn't trusted your father like I did."

She nods.

"I dug up information about him and I didn't want to

meet him until I saw him, both of you, in the news holding the lottery ticket. I followed him pretty much everywhere to learn more about him. I looked him up and found out he was married. Or remarried, I guess. But when I found out he was married to Lynn Miller, I looked you up, too, and it didn't take long for me to work out that you were my mother. Maybe I would have done it earlier had I known you'd kept your maiden name. But I didn't know what it was. My parents—my adopted parents—didn't know."

A sudden memory, like a fog lifting, comes to mind. A woman asking me to sign a paper, information scribbled on it, none of it clear what exactly it is. But now I understand. It was the adoption papers I'd promised to give my daughter to a family who could care for her. Another proof I was a terrible person, a terrible mother, someone who failed her own child. I push the memory away and focus on what is in front of me.

I nod as she tells me her side of the tale, and I feel proud of her persistence and intelligence. But then I'm struck with another sudden thought.

"Was it you who left the notes in front of my house?"

She nods. "Yes." She looks down at our entangled hands, then looks up at me. "I've been trying to send you some sign that I was alive and looking for you, but I guess I didn't do a good job."

"I ... I never would have thought of it. You left a voodoo doll on my steps, so I definitely didn't think of it as a good sign. My first thought was that someone wanted me dead."

She widens her eyes, then laughs. "No. That wasn't a

voodoo doll. That was just a baby toy, another clue about your child, me. I thought maybe you'd get it."

I shake with embarrassment, cringing at the frenzy and paranoia I'd got caught up in after my win.

"I feel so stupid."

"Don't," she says. "It wasn't easy for me, either. I met Jimmy the day after you appeared on the news. He denied being my father and wanted nothing to do with me. When I asked him about you, he insisted you were dead. And I think I might have heard him say 'or soon will be.' I couldn't help but think he was going to hurt you."

I shake my head. "Why didn't you just come and meet me? Why did you follow me everywhere?"

"Because ... because I was afraid."

"Afraid of what?"

"That you might kill me." Lucy stares at me with menacing eyes.

I feel a jab in my stomach. I yank my hands out of hers and pull back. "Listen. It wasn't my fault I didn't find you. Your father lied. He led me to believe you didn't survive."

She gives me a crooked smile. "You believed that piece of shit, eh? You stayed with him even though he treated you like a useless dirty rag. What the fuck is wrong with you?"

I want to ask her how she knew all these things, but does it even matter?

"Your father was too controlling." My voice sounds whiny. "I had no choice—"

"Everybody has a choice when they want it. But you

didn't. You didn't give a shit about changing your life and getting away from him, to become a better person."

I swallow a lump in my throat and my palms drenched in sweat. This is taking a dark turn. This isn't how I want things to go.

"I'm sorry. I'm so sorry."

She casts a wide smile and says, "It's okay. Don't worry. You're only human." Her voice changes again, back into a singsong tone, and her mood lightens instantaneously.

"Please know I want to do better." I say. "I'll give you all my money. And I just put an offer down on a house. You can have it all," I blurt out.

She sews her eyebrows together. "I guess that's fine. But money won't make up for all the years of not knowing you."

"I know."

"My adopted mother died a couple of years ago. A heart attack." She shrugs. "I miss her and hope to have you in my life."

"Yes, love."

She flinches at the pet name I just called her. It had fallen out naturally, full of heart. To my relief, it puts a smile on her face.

"All I ever wanted is to be loved and accepted and have a happy family."

"We can be that. It's not too late." I don't tell her I am dying or that Jimmy is lying cut in pieces at the bottom of the ocean. But it's good to have it for at least a little while. I remain hopeful.

"Mom, please hug me."

I stare at her, overwhelmed at the request. She wants my hug, for my body to wrap her up. I come close to her and place one hand around her neck. I feel the goosebumps on her skin. It's getting colder, and the sky is getting cloudier, and the ocean stronger and wilder. We sit on the sand for a while, holding each other, whispering stories, sharing the times we have lost the past twenty-five years. We laugh together and give occasional kisses on the cheek.

I ask her what her favorite food is, whether she has a boyfriend, and any quirks she wants to share with me. We giggle as we discover silly things about each other, and I can't believe how many similarities we have. We're having so much fun. I forget that time is passing us by. It feels like it's standing still, and the Earth has stopped moving.

By the time we get to know our deepest secrets, desires, and dreams, the sun slides down the horizon. The darkness envelops us like a gentle blanket around our skin. We sit motionless, embracing each other and inhaling deep breaths, as we look forward to welcoming the beckoning of a new day.

Thank you for reading! Stay tuned for Part 2 - coming out next year!

ACKNOWLEDGMENTS

As an indie author, I don't get to work with an army of people it takes to produce a book. But there are several people who have been instrumental in my writing journey I'd like to thank. Writing can be difficult and lonely, and sometimes, we writers need to be reassured that our words are meaningful, and not a waste of time. A trusting circle is important, and I am happy to know I have it.

Jessica Ryn, your editing skills are unparalleled. I am so grateful to you for making my books polished and shiny. I have full confidence in myself, and pushing the "publish" button when the time comes becomes easier because of you. Thank you for all your great comments and edits. You are brilliant!

Thanks to my friend, Melisa Delibegovic, who has read every single book of mine and whose hawk eye catches even the smallest typo. I appreciate your willingness to read through my books and give me an honest opinion. I am so happy to have a great friend like you.

A million thanks to my husband, Chad Vecitis, who got me started with writing as my second career. I appreciate your support, encouragement, and objectiveness in this competitive and never-ending changing vocation. You are my rock, and I love you to the moon and back.

My little munchkin, who melts all my problems away in his presence, I am so grateful you exist in this world. You are the sunshine whose rays reach distant galaxies. You are the most inquisitive, fun-loving, and funniest three-year-old I've known, and I am so glad to call you my son. I love you so much; it hurts.

A zillion thanks to the members of the Psychological Thriller Readers group on Facebook. I love how supportive and kind you are to budding authors like myself. Because of you, this book has gotten some attention before it even came out! You have made a readers community like no other group has done, and I love all the internal jokes you make along the way (IYKYK)! You make me laugh.

Thank you, reader, for giving this book a chance and reading it to the end. I know books are read subjectively, but I hope it gave you some escape from the real world and had you entertained.

THANK YOU

I sincerely thank you for reading this book!

Please consider leaving a review, even if it's only a sentence, checking out my other books, and subscribing to my website. I'm also happy to answer any questions you may have, so do please get in touch with me via my website:

https://nadijamujagic.com

SUBSCRIBE

If you'd like to keep up to date with my latest releases, or get news about occasional free or discounted books, please sign up at the link below. We'll never share your email address and you can unsubscribe anytime:

https://nadijamujagic.com

ABOUT THE AUTHOR

Nadija Mujagić was born and raised in Sarajevo, Bosnia and Herzegovina, what used to be the former Yugoslavia back in the late 1970s. In 1997, she moved to the United States shortly after the end of the Bosnian War and has lived in Massachusetts since. In her spare time, she enjoys playing sports and electric bass guitar. *Lottery of Secrets* is her seventh book.

ALSO BY NADIJA MUJAGIC

Ten Thousand Shells and Counting: A Memoir
Immigrated: A Memoir
Till a Better World: Woman's Fiction
The Brilliant Mirage: A Thriller
The Exchange: A Psychological Thriller
The Master of Demise: A Psychological Thriller